The

Professor

A Temptation Press Anthology

The Professor

A Temptation Press Anthology

TEMPTATION
PRESS

Acknowledgements

Temptation Press would like to thank all those that contributed to this anthology. We chose to showcase four new voices that best represented our vision for this work.

We would also like to thank our Temptation Press team for all their dedication and hard work to these projects.

Contents

A Winter's Tale

Catherine J. Wright

Is there anything more inspiring
To a certain kind of bluestocking
Than a man who speaks in pentameter
And makes apt allusions to Demeter
Brashly uses the word 'imbroglio'
Conjures Hamlet and evokes Romeo
With a play from the Bard across his knee
For she thinks, *"Dear God, why isn't that me?"*

"Cathy!" Anne exclaims; the corners of her mouth are deepening, though she's doing her best to look annoyed as she flops down on her bed opposite me. "You can't actually print that. Even the Midwestern University Standard has… well—standards."

"Why not? It doesn't contain one of George Carlin's seven words."

Anne gives me her best Spock eyebrow. Her ability to call bullshit was one of the things that drew us together freshman year. "For starters," she said, "he'll know."

I redden a little. "Why would he bother reading the student paper? I mean, I contribute, and I don't read it." But at the mere possibility of his reading it did my heart fly.

"Don't you have an actual paper to write?" she asks, waggling a finger at me and grinning.

"I started. I put my name, the course title, and the date in the header."

"Oh, God."

"I've got a lot of latitude for this one. It can be on any theme spanning five or more plays, except 'religion in Shakespeare,' 'feminism in Shakespeare,' and 'suicide in Shakespeare.' He says they're done to death, and he'll dock anyone who chooses those topics a full letter grade from the get-go."

"Ouch."

"Hey, he's tough but fair."

"And this is your dreamboat?"

"Yes, exactly," I grin. "My theme is going to be 'unrequited love.'"

"Subtlety, thy name is Cathy."

But in the end, there is only so much one term paper, even one for *him*, can lean on Ophelia.

Ophelia, I've always felt, deserved her own emo high school TV spinoff. She would be a beautiful-but-nearsighted introvert who's into botany. Hamlet would be a track and field star—because obviously, he can't decide between the two. But I digress.

I flirt with talking about sex across comedies, histories, and tragedies outright—*all those pilgrim hands touching!*—but then hit on something slightly more nuanced: *female desire in Shakespeare. Juliet and her pubescent longings, and Hamlet's cougar mother Gertrude, obviously; but also, Richard III's wooed-and-won corpse-side, Anne. The 'if-you-can't-beat-'em-make-'em-laugh' Beatrice. God knows Desdemona and Othello were hot and heavy before things just got … heavy.*

And, look! There's Ophelia again—I picture her playing a desultory game of catch with Laertes on their street lit lawn; he's the theatre-nerd hero who screams at Hamlet to "Stay away from my sister!" in the episode before the Christmas break— *There're five women. Shit, Gertrude and Ophelia are both from the same play. Viola, maybe? Ugh, no. All I can picture is an overwrought Gwyneth Paltrow on an island.*

I briefly imagine being shipwrecked with Tim on some faraway isle, after some dreadful tempest. Then I picture a calmer scene, in *From Here to Eternity*-cerulean tones. *He'd be lying half-in, half-out of the waves, with me beside him, my head nestled in the hollow between his neck and shoulder as we …*

Maybe all of my borrowed characters could live in the same town—fair Verona, obviously. The show would revolve around Ophelia's coming-of-age, although one major plotline would be all of the Sam-and-Diane-ness between her and Hamlet. She would probably be friends with Jessica from The Merchant of Venice, whose house would be vandalized by neo-Nazis after her father bankrupts the descendant of the town founder, and Miranda from The Tempest, who would arrive in the brave new world that is Verona High when her unconventional and widowed father, Tom Prospero, becomes the principal.

Obviously, one of his first challenges on the job would be Jimmy Caliban, an ex-gang member who challenges Prospero's so-called 'wisdom'—especially when Miranda develops a crush on him. Prospero, in turn, would have an ambiguous relationship with the mysteriously androgynous Ariel, who—

"I'm calling it," says Anne, pulling on her nightshirt and yawning gratuitously. "Maybe next time you could consider starting your paper more than twelve hours ahead of the deadline."

"Just because you're a responsible young adult doesn't mean we all are."

"Good night," she smiles.

"Good night," I say.

I will not turn Verona into *Ten Things I Hate About You*, redux. It'll be more like *Dynasty*. *Ooh, I haven't even gotten to the Macbeths. One percenters, of course; she would host glamorous key parties and make him watch, I bet.*

My clock is flashing 1:37. Shit.

By dawn, I have a term paper. And forty-seven ideas for a pilot scribbled in my purple notebook. *And fifty doodled hearts in the margins.*

I sleep for precisely three hours until Anne's alarm goes off at the crack of 9:45. Between us, I think we hit all seven of George Carlin's words, and manage to shower/brush teeth/shove in dry cereal/cross campus in time for our 10:30 classes. A quick early lunch, and then the pièce de résistance at 12:30.

Dr. Timothy Reynolds, with his prematurely grey hair and British accent and Darcy-esque good looks, has hit the trifecta to win my clichéd Anglophile heart. His being a professor is just a bonus. His finger accidentally brushes mine when he collects the papers, and my cheeks begin radiating Day-Glo pink.

I pointed him out to Anne once as we walked across campus. "He's too old for you," she declared.

"He's a silver fox!" I retorted.

My kingdom for a seat in his course!

I can see lean muscle rippling beneath his simple button-down white shirt. I lose the thread of the lecture for a moment, listening to the pure and lilting cadences of the BBC, right here in the uninspired center of the upper Midwest. *And those eyes! The gods may have dipped them in the great pool of an azure sky … or perhaps they were painted by some half-mad Renaissance artist who spent his entire salary on lapis lazuli to grind into a holy tincture for Mary's robes …*

Tim describes Hamlet's craft and wit in using theatre to prick his stepfather's conscience, while I try not to stare. "The play's the thing," Tim concludes.

The hour has gone, and any actual content from the lecture has entered my consciousness through osmosis, if at all. *Parting is indeed a sweet sorrow! I won't get to see those gorgeous eyes for another two days …*

Except.

"Catherine, may I see you for a moment?"

Yes, yes, yes. How much of me would you like to see?

"Have you got a class after this?"

"Not until four thirty."

We walk out of the classroom, side by side; I am happily aware that my head would fall against his shoulder just as I always imagined. We arrive at his office a few moments later; it contains a marble bust of W.S. himself and neat stacks of papers at ninety-degree angles to the corners of his desk.

Tim sits, and steeples his hands, harkening back rather delightfully to Dumbledore—Richard Harris edition—and Robin Williams in Dead Poets Society.

"I'd like you to do something for me."

Certainly. Even if it's illegal in twelve states.

"I'd like you to write an essay comparing and contrasting any two characters from Hamlet and Macbeth."

That is not precisely what I'd hoped to hear.

"Wh- what?"

"It's an … extra assignment. You have forty-five minutes."

I choose Banquo and Hamlet, both of whom are hell-bent on evoking some display of awareness, some recognition, from the kings in their lives—but with staggeringly different levels of culpability themselves, I might add—and start writing.

Banquo, I think, would appear on the show—not dead, but perhaps wrongfully imprisoned for a white-collar crime that Macbeth committed after peremptorily ousting his company's CEO, while his son Fleance leaves home to find himself like a tacky beat poet … focus, Cathy; focus.

I set down the final period just as the timer on Tim's watch goes off, and I hand him my paper, wary, exultant.

He reads it, his finely wrought mouth is set. I manage to contain myself, and to refrain from grabbing him by the shoulders and demanding, "What is going on?"—but only just. Because his shoulders are marvelously sculpted, like the prototype for David.

He sets down the paper. "This is good," he says. His elegantly restrained expression threatens to transport me; in American English, that would be praise of the highest order. "I'm so sorry to have wasted your time."

I am self-conscious enough to recognize that it is impossible to furrow one's brow and still look passably attractive, so I simply try to appear interested, in three-quarter profile.

"Your last essay showed that you are head and shoulders above the rest," he says, and my heart performs a complicated Bossa Nova while I pretend to smile modestly. "I wasn't certain that you had written it without … help. Clearly, I was wrong." He looks charmingly apologetic. "Perhaps I can buy you a coffee to atone in some way."

YES. THANK YOU, O GOD, YES.

"That would be very generous of you."

Off we go, hopping into his vintage black Corvette—because, of course—and we're off to Buzz, the self-consciously indie bookstore/caffeine purveyor downtown. There is one spot left on the street, and Tim's rapid and masterful parallel parking job gives rise to several fleeting gothic fantasies imagining what else he might be able to park, and where.

"What else do you write?" he asks.

"What makes you think I don't just regurgitate literary analysis?"

He grins. "No one who writes like you do limits herself to that."

So, I tell him about my creations, my derivative poetry, and the slightly better short stories, and he tells me about his 'dreadful' novella, which he—with typical British understatement—describes as a poor mash-up of Tennyson and Truman Capote. I picture Guinevere strumming a lute and singing *Moon River* to Lancelot, and this is what emerges from my mouth before I can stop myself.

He laughs. "That sounds better than what I've actually done—but perhaps you'd like to read it." He sips his cappuccino. "Another day, maybe. I understand you have a class."

I make an indifferent noise.

He puts his hand on my arm.

I emit a very different sort of noise, very low. It might almost be described as a purr.

I hope the couple at the next table are as blind as winged Cupid because I recognize the girl from my chemistry lab, and Tim and I are in plain violation of at least three sections of the university's ethics code.

If I'm lucky, we'll break seven.

Twenty minutes later we're at his apartment, which is neat and comfortable and lined with books. I like this place and willingly could waste my time in it. Anne would call it an intrinsic reproach to my half of the dorm room, which is littered with the detritus of my genius, and dirty laundry.

This is what Shakespeare's own apartment would look like if he were alive today, and had an iMac.

Tim takes my hand, and the spark of his touch radiates directly from my palm to my heart to my stomach to a full five fathoms below. "May I?" he asks.

I press my lips to his in answer and commit us to this pretty folly. He is—I think—surprised, but he wraps his powerful arms around me. His lips are honey and wine, and I am mad-drunk—waxing poetic all at once.

We break this kiss, finally, and our eyes find each other's—shyly.

"Are you—" he begins, and then reddens. "I—oh, God, Catherine … I shouldn't—"

Has not every flawed hero said the same? This is irresistible.

"This lady is not protesting too much," I say, and kiss him again.

And again.

And again.

His tongue enters my mouth, and I draw it in. We are joined, two fusing into one, the inevitable coupling; he murmurs nonsense, calling me his dark lady, then puts his mouth back to mine; he releases a groan that contains all the inevitability of his succumbing. He cups my breast, clinging to it like a drowning man to a spar, and my hand has found its way onto his muscular back. I press myself against him, feel a delightful bulge pressing back.

"Tempt not a desperate man," he murmurs, helplessly.

I respond by leaning forward on tiptoe and dropping my lips to the sweet skin of his neck.

Shall I compare Tim to a summer's day? He is more lovely and less temperate …

That's how it goes, surely.

His skin is warm to the touch, his cool apartment, and it is all I can do not to … *oh, screw it.*

To be, or not to be, naked, that is the question …

I remove his shirt so quickly that the buttons spray into the air, opalescent plastic fireworks, and run my fingers along his magnificent abs. *My God! Every gorgeous muscle is exquisitely defined …*

He—no less eager—strips away my sweater and my t-shirt, until my push-up bra displays my breasts in all their balconetted glory. Then my Romeo's silver head is bent over my chest, as he kisses the tops of my breasts, caresses them, and seeks out the starred prizes within … he draws me into his mouth, and I gasp …

In no time my bra is on the floor too, and he is alternately nuzzling, licking, and suckling my breasts, as my toes curl in my shoes. I am a great ocean, swelling …

I unzip his pants and pull them down.

There he is—measure for measure, glorious in every dimension … I fall to my knees and begin my worship.

My love's richer than my tongue.

I curl my tongue around the head, and draw my mouth up and down his divine girth, until he moans, and falls against the wall. Then he gently touches my cheek.

"What kind of host would I be," he murmurs, "if I did not welcome my guest?"

He walks me over to the bed, and playfully throws me down; I am lying down with my legs dangling over the edge. Without hesitation, he kneels, slides down my panties, lifts up my skirt, and—oh …

Love sought is good, but given unsought, is better.

He slides his tongue up … and down … and in … and I nearly scream, ecstatic from the sudden sharp joy of it. He slides his tongue in and out with a sonneteer's precision, as every muscle in my body screams for sweet release.

Can one desire too much of a good thing?

I am not ready to fulfill my destiny just yet, and I take a moment to remove what little remains of my clothing. "Take me," I whisper.

He, being a perfect gentleman, obliges, and promptly buries his sword to the hilt. He grins, pulls away, and then that glorious girth is again within me.

Now I understand why they call it the beast with two backs; he drives into me, insistently, and I pull him into me, feel his powerful member filling me with contentment, impaling me deliciously, touching my core and stealing my breath away. Then I roll him over, and I ride him, desperately, my breasts swinging wildly over his face, concentrating only on the burgeoning wave within me—and my back arches as that perfect satiation of my lust washes over me.

Three energetic pumps later and he too is spasming, calling on God, all His angels, and Shakespeare's ghost to bear witness to the height of his pleasure.

We lie together, giddy and unembarrassed. I feel gloriously spent.

"Spectacular," he murmurs.

"No argument," I return. "And perhaps in a bit, you can give me my sin again."

We drift off, both of us, perchance to dream, in the somnolent afternoon light.

⊱ ❁ ⊰

I wake first, and dress, while a small smile keeps tugging at the corner of my lips.

He looks impossibly handsome while sleeping, his silver hair and boyish expression in charming contrast.

As he dozes in the fading winter sunlight, I drift toward his computer and shake the mouse awake. There it is, *A Tru Story of the Grail*. A bit puckish for my taste, but adequate.

I read.

It's a time-travel story.

The protagonist's voice is a stilted mélange of blank verse and Tim's ordinarily resonant baritone, occasionally lapsing into a plain replica of Capote's own mellifluous tones. Sometimes midsentence.

Not only is the heroine a Disney cliché, but the entire story fails the Bechdel test.

His vaulting ambition overleaps itself.

I suddenly think I wouldn't mind a shower. Even the fungus-infested showers in my dorm shouldn't be too crowded, this time of day.

When he wakes, I thank him politely for a lovely afternoon and start retrieving my clothes. He looks unhappily bewildered. "Catherine?"

I smile reassuringly. "It really was great." I pause. "I, ah, started your novella."

"It's crap," he reiterates.

I don't have the wherewithal to contradict him; to critique that spasmodically adequate opus; to point out the inconsistencies of voice, the wheezing premise, the Punch-and-Judy characters … or even to agree. *There are more things in my lazy misappropriation of Shakespeare's creations than are dreamt of in his philosophy …*

"I'm teaching Shakespeare 302 next semester," he says. There is a plaintive splinter in his voice that decides the matter.

"I … think I'm going to sign up for screenwriting," I say.

I dress and depart forthwith. I'm no longer thinking about that shower; my fingers are itching for the sweet percussive touch of my laptop. *Richard III has to be part of Verona. Obviously, he's desperate to become the state governor … so he decides to get rid of his chief Republican rival and make a move on the man's longtime partner, Anne Neville—the daughter of the town scion, and Ophelia's favorite teacher at Verona High …*

That's it—Richard's murder of Governor Edward Westminster—and Ophelia's crazy-making discovery of it—would be the season one finale!

When I return to my room, I type in the header: Pilot: Fair Verona.

This above all, to mine own self I must be true.

Bulletproof

Brandon French

He was a big guy, hulking and round-shouldered, with thick glasses, chipped brown teeth, and a beard as scraggly as an unwatered lawn. According to the university's Extension Catalogue, he'd been teaching this Advanced Fiction class for twenty-seven years and was voted *Best Instructor* twice.

He spent the first half of the three-hour class talking about himself. Third of eight children. Irish Catholic. Raised by a school-teacher mother, no mention of a father. Immaculate conception? Working-class family, used to be an auto mechanic. Eventually decided to become a writer. Went through the MFA Program at Iowa. The famous one. Big deal. Favorite short-story writers: Flannery O'Connor, Robert Stone,

Flannery O'Connor, Denis Johnson, Raymond Carver, Flannery O'Connor. Okay, got it. Mentioned his wife Trudie, a CPA who writes poetry. Mentioned awards, the usual—Pushcart, O'Henry. But no New Yorker. No Paris Review. No Best American Short Stories. Made me wonder if Bill Keogh was second-rate. Made me suspect he was a narcissistic asshole. *What have I gotten myself into,* I wondered, *ten nighttime marathons with a blowhard, after an exhausting day in Business Affairs at Sony?*

I glanced around at my classmates, seven men and five women, all of them younger than I was, although one chatty woman looked to be in her mid-forties. Supposedly, we were all 'advanced,' having had to email Keogh a writing sample to get in, except for the repeaters who'd already taken the class with him a couple of times. But I had my doubts about the talent level after reading 'Russian Dressing,' the first story we were going to discuss after the fifteen-minute break. It was about the emotional impact of a young man's visit to Moscow, but it could just as well have been a visit to Cleveland, the way it was written.

Keogh began by asking the writer, a twenty-something with a neck as long as pulled taffy, one question, "How did it smell in the cab that took you from the airport to your hotel?"

All of a sudden, taffy-neck remembered the upholstery's mildewed stench, the driver's garlicky breath, his violent assaults on the car horn as he hurled Slavic curses at other drivers and slow-footed pedestrians, the bumps and potholes in the road, and the ancient auto's groaning transmission.

Wow.

I recognized the real deal when I saw it. Bill Keogh was the real deal. Not that this would keep me from disparaging him down the road, but I'm getting ahead of myself. At that moment, I was totally smitten.

The next week, it was my turn to present a story, 'My Life to Live,' about a depressed college professor, a relentless vacuum-cleaner salesman and a paranoid friend who thinks the NSA has planted listening devices in his molars.

Keogh said it was well-written and mildly amusing, but it wasn't a story. He would say that often, comparing me to Alice Munro, whose novelistic storytelling he didn't admire.

"You're a victim of autobiography, Ms. de Lucca," he said, tossing his heavily annotated copy back at me. "Serve the story, not the truth."

Once Keogh delivered the death penalty, everybody else followed along like lemmings. It was like having your sleek fighter jet shot out of the sky by Nazis in an old war movie.

Boom. Rat-ta-ta-tat. Splat.

"I'll show HIM!" I vowed, after scraping what was left of my confidence off the pavement.

I extensively revised 'My Life to Live,' and wrote a whole new story every seven days for the next eight weeks, working on them mornings, evenings, and weekends. I also stole time at the office, an advantage of doing the preponderance of my work as a lawyer on a computer. I wrote in my head as I was walking my Labradoodles, Rocco and Zoey, or watching TV, or talking on the phone, hoping nobody I cared about could hear the click-click of the computer keys. I even dreamed revisions, keeping a notebook and pen next to the bed so I could scratch out ideas in the dark.

On the days when I couldn't write, I read. "See what you can steal," Keogh told us, and I took him at his word. I stole from Clare Vaye Watkins and James Joyce, racing back to my computer with the precious booty. I ripped off John Cheever and Alan Gurganus, George Saunders, David Means, Jhumpa Lahiri, and the amazing Lauren Groff—"She is exhausting to everyone. She would take a break from herself, too, but she doesn't have that option." *Is that me, too,* I wondered.

Keogh began referring to me as "the machine," which sounded more like an accusation than a compliment. But I had come to this process late in the game, and I felt a compulsion to capture, and preserve, my past— not only the broad strokes of my parents and childhood but the smallest details of my experience, the mushroomy odor of newborn cats beneath a neighbor's stairway when I was three, the cool, slippery touch of my father's white silk scarf when he and my mother went out for the evening, the still life of an empty neighborhood lot adorned with dandelions and discarded refrigerator boxes.

And like a rapacious plant, I was fed and watered by each exclamation point Keogh left in the margins, indicating that he liked a sentence, or sometimes a whole paragraph. I even treasured his 'Not too bad, pretty good, kiddo,' and 'Keep going with this.' But there was also 'Lazy writing, You missed the boat,' and 'B-o-r-i-n-g,' which hit me like slaps and punches.

By the time the quarter ended, I had nine finished stories, one of which, 'The Lion Queen,' a fiercely comic account of working for a tyrant at MGM, Keogh declared bulletproof—after three major revisions and two polishes.

"Bulletproof is the goal," Keogh said, derived from his experience as a journal editor in northern California. "A dull opening," he warned, "or a lame image, or even a couple of typos are ample reason to reject a story. And that's what the guy wants—an excuse to toss it and get on to the next eighty he has to read. Because there he is, still in his bathrobe at noon, hungover, depressed, and pissed off that his latest book has crapped out or still hasn't found a publisher."

We looked at each other and laughed, we couldn't help it, the description sounded so much like Keogh.

"Ship 'Lion Queen' off to a few places," Keogh called out as I was leaving the classroom for the winter break. "It'll be good practice."

I hoarded his encouragement like the last gulp of water in my canteen, hoping it would get me through the three-month hiatus until his spring class began. I was afraid that, without Keogh, I wouldn't be able to function. He had become my muse, my maestro, and after a single semester, I'd surrendered most of my confidence as a writer to him.

Around Valentine's Day, I forwarded Keogh an email from a small journal, whose themed issue was 'The Seven Deadly Sins.' The editors loved 'The Lion Queen,' and wanted to publish it as an example of Wrath. I felt like I'd just been nominated for a Pulitzer.

'The Lion Queen' by Monserat de Lucca.

Holy shit.

How can you not love the person who helps you get your first publication? How can you not believe that your mentor has the magic juju that will carry you to fame and—well, fame. There's surely no fortune to be made writing short stories unless you're one of The New Yorker's darlings. Or you're Philip K. Dick, and Steven Spielberg wants to turn 'The Minority Report' into a movie.

But what I felt for Keogh wasn't love-love, not that lust-charged lunacy that infected me like a bad bout of flu and made my whole body ache with longing. It was more like the childhood passion I felt for my father, Romaine de Lucca, a renowned translator of Dante whom I idolized as a little girl. He was my first, and best, teacher. He introduced me to the beauty of literature, fine art, and classical music before a heart attack took him when I was twenty.

Falling in love with my teachers had become commonplace for me, especially in college. But my longing was unrequited until my senior-year Renaissance lit class with Asher Hachuk, a scrappy, charismatic Russian Jew, whose book 'Sin and Salvation,' about Spenser's 'The Faerie Queen,' was an academic best seller.

Despite being married—as they all were—Asher kissed me passionately in cars, closets, and dark hallways, until we ended up in my bed. That's where we remained for the next four years, fucking and fighting, mostly over his infidelities, until I finished law school and his first wife divorced him. Soon after that, Asher proposed to a worshipful graduate student who'd been copy editing his new book, 'Chaucer's Divine Decadence,' and I found my way into another tumultuous relationship, this time with a married TV producer at MGM named Ken.

Ken convinced me to write a salacious novel about my college escapades, 'The Professors' Groupie,' which featured an amorous undergrad named Roxanne and a chorus line of professors, including a brilliant Russian Jewish intellectual named Seymour Gold. But even though I had a New York agent, thanks to a deal my production company made optioning a best seller, my novel's fragmented postmodern narrative, for which I blame John Barth and Thomas Pynchon, was apparently too daunting to market, especially from an unknown writer, and while a couple of prestigious publishers admired it, neither of them took it on.

I stopped writing fiction for a couple of decades until another bad break-up, and a celebrated screenwriter who accused me of 'galactic misrepresentation' in his deal memo, propelled me into Keogh's seminar.

In retrospect, it's not surprising that Keogh's class became my central passion. The denuding of my personal life had occurred so gradually that I'd failed to notice the divestment—like when the soapy water slowly drains out of your bath, and you don't realize it until you're left naked and goose-pimpled in an empty tub.

My friends had married, divorced, and married again. They had birthed children who needed to be chauffeured to gymnastics, soccer practice, and private tutoring. Others had moved to exotic realms like North Carolina and Montana.

My mother, in the last few years before she died, swallowed up most of my free time. She'd had a stroke, which caused her to ask the same questions again and again. When can I leave the nursing home? Who took my (yellow, green, apricot) sweater? Why did you boycott your father's funeral? But we still enjoyed our Sunday afternoons listening to opera on the radio, and sometimes I'd bring her to my condo for one of my father's culinary specialties—Osso Bucco, ground lamb manicotti, or risotto with wild mushrooms, which he'd taught me how to prepare when I was a child.

Other factors also contributed to my obsession with Keogh's class. After my mother's death, I became overly fond of alcohol and used it to battle a chronic depression, which led to grave household neglect and several bouts of compulsive online spending. My condo grew so cluttered and untended that the only visitors I permitted were the occasional plumber or handyman. Perhaps that's the way I wanted it— an excuse to barricade myself from the outside world.

But after an embarrassing incident at the Century City Mall, where I passed out and had to be ambulanced to UCLA Emergency, I spent time in rehab, joined AA and finally decided, albeit tentatively, to rejoin the living. Hence Keogh's class. The writing, it turned out, was therapeutic, giving me a forum for many of the emotions I had struggled to suppress.

"Why did you use the second person?" Keogh asked during the class discussion of 'Fallen,' a story inspired by my bout with alcoholism.

"The narrator needs to keep the nightmare at arm's length so it can be funny as well as harrowing," I said. "It's a defense mechanism."

"Good answer. I usually hate the second person, it seems so gimmicky and intrusive, but I think it works in this case."

'Fallen' was my fourth story to be published in a journal, getting snapped up in less than three weeks. I was on a roll, I exulted, as long as I kept writing. I felt like the sorcerer's apprentice, or the ballerina in 'The Red Shoes,' fated to write ceaselessly and doomed if I didn't. But during my third quarter with Keogh, things began to go south.

Keogh had become increasingly resentful of my compulsion to provide a complete story for every homework assignment, sometimes as long as fifteen or twenty pages. Each week he reiterated that he only wanted a few pages, just the seed of a story we could grow on our own after the quarter ended. And each week I ignored him.

"Certain people," he said with a menacing smile, "are determined to write, and to make me read, 'War and Peace' every seven days."

Smiling back at him, I pretended that he was kidding. I rationalized that turning in a few pages was like offering someone two apples and a cup of flour and saying, "This might eventually be a pie." But I exploited him mercilessly, craving his input and approval like a junkie.

By my fourth quarter with Keogh, eight of my stories had been accepted for publication—seven more than anyone else in the class. But my success, contrary to my expectations, had not made me one of Keogh's favorites, not one of the chosen people he used to chat up before class and during the breaks—bantering about cars, sports, and cooking. He was a Marcella Hazan aficionado, as my father had been. Nor did it provoke an invitation to Keogh's home group, which met at his house every two weeks, year-round, to critique one another's writing.

When I asked him about it, he was evasive, saying, "It's just a bunch of friends who've known each other for decades." But that, I learned, was a lie. Keogh had invited Alida, a pretty young Latina whose work he said was "brilliant," to join, and Tommy, a professional photographer who looked like Johnny Depp and wrote juicy stories about working as a PA at a San Fernando Valley porn production company.

"In the little world where children have their existence," Charles Dickens wrote, "there is nothing so finely perceived, or so finely felt, as an injustice." Keogh's favoritism, not to mention the lie, yanked my legs out from under me and loosed a monstrous anger. I felt entitled to be in his home group, and I hated him for excluding me.

"Why doesn't he like me?" I asked Tanya, one of the repeaters I'd become friendly with.

"You're too advanced. He likes the babies who he can help get into MFA programs, you know, the ones who think he's God and hang on every word he says."

Her comment stung me, although I knew it was probably true. But how could she possibly understand how I felt? She was married and pregnant with her first child. I was single, childless and perimenopausal.

"He teaches the same stories every quarter," I complained in the hallway during breaks. "He tells the same personal anecdotes, gives the exact same homework assignments, and he caters to his pets shamelessly, even when their stories are lousy!"

None of the repeaters disagreed with me, but they just shrugged it off. They probably thought I was a spoiled, cranky baby, waa-waa-waa, especially since my stories kept getting published. I knew I was being unfair. Flaws aside, Bill Keogh read and critiqued more homework, reviewed more revisions, and elevated the skills of more fiction writers than any other teacher in the writers' program, grumbling about it bitterly, yes, toward the end of each quarter, but never lightening his load. What did I want from him, for Christ sake? That was the sixty-four-thousand-dollar question, and the only answer I could come up with was, *more*.

For the next year, I courted Keogh shamelessly, crocheting scarves and blankets for him, bringing him lemons and limes from my patio fruit trees, sending him an expensive rare book that he'd coveted, even making him a sweatshirt with Joan Didion's famous one-liner, 'Writers are always selling somebody out.' He seemed a little gentler after receiving these burnt offerings, a little less sarcastic and irritable about my relentless output, with a greater willingness to talk to me during class breaks about MFA programs—"Should I pursue one?" "You don't need it," he said—or the latest book on the Catholic-priest scandals, "Too painful," he said.

He even shared an anecdote about Raymond Carver at a reading of his latest short story collection, "That's no good," Carver said about a particular word he'd written, I don't remember what it was, but he was pissed off at himself for not catching it before publication. Then he pulled out a pen and scribbled a better choice in the margin.

"So much for bulletproof," I said, and Keogh chuckled.

"'Forget your perfect offering, there's a crack in everything, that's how the light gets in,'" he said.

"Thank God for Leonard Cohen."

But our conversations never delighted Keogh like the ones he carried on with his pets, and then there was the dreadful mishap with an email.

Keogh had been especially solicitous to a languorous young beauty named Kelly, whose long blond curtain of hair kept falling over one eye like a 1940's noir actress. He invariably found her mediocre writing full of promise, and he tolerated and excused her chronic lateness in completing assignments.

This classroom romance tormented me as if Keogh were my lover, and when we didn't receive Kelly's twenty-page story until a day before class, I wrote a scathing email with the subject line, 'Keogh's Outrageous Favoritism.'

"Why should we have to kowtow to Kelly's narcissistic flouting of the rules just because she gives Keogh a hard-on?" I wrote. "He has a lot of fucking nerve!"

The message went out to the entire class, excepting Kelly. But I made the fatal error of using the classroom email chain, so it also reached Keogh.

When I spotted him in the parking lot the next evening on my way to class, his face was contorted with rage.

"Stay away from me, de Lucca," he rumbled, like the drumroll of thunder before a deluge. "You're lucky I don't kick you out."

"I'm sorry," I said, "please, please, don't make me—"

"What the fuck is wrong with you?" he said, cutting me off with a menacing wave of his hand.

"I don't know," I said, bursting into tears. "I really don't know."

I sent Keogh several apologies over the next week, none of which generated a response, so I was left struggling to salvage our relationship for the remainder of the quarter. I went out of my way to be deferential to him whenever I spoke in class, offering, rather than asserting, opinions and withholding any disagreements. But whatever goodwill I had managed to cultivate over the first four quarters was obliterated by my scurrilous email.

Nonetheless, Keogh nominated my story, 'Crash and Burn,' for the annual Curt Johnson Fiction Prize which, a month later, it won. Then he kicked me out. His last email said, "You've read it all, heard it all, and learned as much as I can teach you. Time to move on."

'Crash and Burn' was about my father. When I was twenty, I had discovered him lying across his large office desk at Columbia on top of a willowy young blond with a Roman nose and translucent ivory skin. I'd had the intention of treating him to lunch while we were both on Christmas break. He was supposed to have been working on a new translation of La Vita Nuova, about Beatrice, the lifelong object of Dante's ardor—*Bay-a-treech-ay*, as my father pronounced it, in the elegant Italian way.

In 'Crash and Burn,' the narrator wonders if the blonde was her father's Bay-a-treech-ay, the symbol of salvation in The Divine Comedy, while her mother, like Dante's wife, was merely a respectable pretense. Perhaps there had been a long parade of Bay-a-treech-ays, the narrator speculates, now that her exalted image of her father has been irreparably tarnished. Perhaps the father she'd adored was a serial philanderer, a phony, a manikin in an exquisitely tailored suit, who'd fooled her for the first twenty years of her life. Like a jilted lover, she refuses to see him afterward, or talk to him on the phone, and she sets fire to the letter he sends her without reading it.

The father is discovered by a neighbor on New Year's Day, a lonely specter lying dead next to his car. His patrician features and lion's mane of dense black and white hair are as frozen in place as the head of a Roman statue, toppled like the ruins of Ozymandias.

"You've nailed it," Keogh wrote on the last page of the manuscript, "but what about the fate of a daughter who kills off her father? That should keep you writing for a while."

Reckless

Nicole Bea

Bishop and I were broken from the moment we met until the moment we fell apart.

He loved autumn, rock and roll, and me. I loved the sound the world made when we were alone together. And him. Of course, I loved him. Absolutely and ardently.

It all started and ended in a matter of weeks, a late-fall fling that spanned the month of November, the undressing of trees, and the first snowfall. He was the first person I met at Fischer-Fleming University that I thought may have been boyfriend material, the appealing thought of a brewing relationship pleasing my mind. But he was also the last person I would have thought would break my heart, as naive as the whole prospect sounds.

The whole thing was furious, a tempest, raging between hormones and time constraints and the fear of the unknown. The recipe for an absolutely beautiful disaster.

In hindsight, I can't decide if I wish I would have had a sign. I'm not sure I would have listened to it anyway.

There are no bells in university to tell you when a class is over, no warning that the period is coming to an end. Everyone sort of just starts packing up their things slowly, hoping nobody will notice, praying the professor won't keep talking, thinking about what percentage of their body is made up of coffee. Five days a week, multiple times per day classes would pull this unconscious routine as a collective group, working off separate individual calendars. The last few minutes are comprised of a feeling, a need to move on, a glance at a watch or a glimpse of a clock—and then the mass rises for their next engagement. Group Dynamics; Sociology 101.

The bigger the group, the stronger the actions and reactions.

But Bishop and I? We were a dyad—the most volatile of dynamics—and true to definition, we were akin to fireworks.

I can't find pretty enough words to tell you what Bishop Gale was to me, but at the time he was made up of at least part nostalgia, one-part conquest, and one-part guy next door. Something about his hair was a relic of my high school obsession with the bad boy, he was built like a lean Greek god, and the simple fact that half of campus and the entirety of our group wanted him spoke to me of one thing: *longing*. Desperate, fervent longing.

November was the month we had together. A crisp, uneven time of patchy trees and sporadic snow that never accumulated into much. Perhaps it was intended as a symbol for our relationship; short, erratic, ever-changing. Or maybe I just read into things too much, and nothing has any fate behind it at all; it remains illogical, random, and unlimited.

I fell for Bishop hard and fast—almost overnight—with the rise of a new tide and the washing out of another. I gave him no time to contemplate his girlfriend, who asked him recently to marry her, though I mentioned her often enough, hoping that perhaps my distraction would be enough to draw him away. I can only assume it was. He can't tell me the difference anymore. So instead, I just make up the ending to the story myself. I must act as my own muse.

Bishop did as he said he would. He texted me after he found out Gemma was cheating on him, exhausted, confirming that her possessions were out of his place and back to her parents on Hawthorne, adjacent to the frat house on Oxford. He continued to refer to it as a convenient change of location, even though I knew a little part of him was dying inside at the loss of his long-time girlfriend. I didn't want to think about it, didn't want to think about her. I wanted to live in a world where only Bishop and I existed.

And so, for a while, I did.

It was a Thursday night, the replacement Friday for students at Fischer-Fleming University as we didn't have scheduled classes on Fridays. I was sitting, half asleep, in my four o'clock Contemporary Sociological Theory class with Professor Wyatt when I felt my phone buzz on my leg. Wyatt had a reputation as a droner—the kind of lecturer that doesn't even look up at the class to make sure the attendees are still alive—and so I checked my phone from my back-row seat with no concerns.

Wanna meet up after class?

　　　　　　　　　Please. What were you thinking?

Walk to North Garden Park?

                    Absolutely. Meet outside CL at 530.

I tucked my phone into the strap of my bag in one fluid motion, the girl beside me barely stirring. There was no telling if she was conscious and listening to Wyatt or if she had passed out long ago. Her chocolate colored hair fell in loose waves over the edge of her desk, a pen upright in her hand but unmoving. I'd have placed my bets on her being asleep, if I were into betting.

I amused myself by staring out the windows to the right of the classroom door, long frames spanning the length of the farthest wall. It was nearly dark out by that time, the nighttime air rolling in on top of the daytime winds, pushing out the light of the sun in exchange for the lauding moon. It was a pretty period on campus, the residences with glowing glass and warmed brick, and the trees rustling tentatively with the bits of leftover autumn in preparation for winter.

Wyatt let us out ten minutes early, I remember because I took the long way around to the Cedar Lounge past the gym and across the empty football field. The campus lights were bright and buzzing in the setting tapestry, a background noise to the sky-bound art that signified the change of time of day.

Bishop met me five minutes late, but I didn't mind and didn't question the difference.

"Hey, Tee." A cigarette hung from Bishop's mouth as he tried to walk and light it at the same time, a fading flame coming from his lighter. It was just enough to get the smoke lit, a red dot in the closing blackness, smoke tendrils oozing up to the atmosphere.

"Bishop. How was class?"

"Uneventful. I'm up to my ears in English Lit. I don't think they can jam any more books into my head before finals." He smiled and handed me the cigarette, my cold fingers brushing against his lukewarm ones.

"Anything I can help with?"

"Doubt it, unless you want to write my exam for me." The statement required no response, and so I didn't bother, instead starting along the path toward the entry to North Garden Park.

We moved along in silence until we reached the gates.

"I think we need to talk," Bishop began, lifting the latch and letting me through the wrought iron barrier. Gravel crunched underneath my feet, emphasizing his point.

"About what?"

"I think I love you."

"You what?" I responded, taken aback at the blunt honesty.

"You heard me. Gemma and I have been an apocalypse long since coming, I like you, and I want to see where this goes." He took a drag of his smoke just then as if relieved that he was able to make his point.

"Are you always this forward?"

He handed the last of the cigarette to me, and I finished it off in one long pull.

"I know what I want, Tee. Doesn't matter if alcohol is involved or not."

I crushed the smoke under my shoe, outing the dregs, and continued walking the park with Bishop at my side. We remained in each other's personal bubbles, brushing against each other occasionally, our fingers dancing around the subject until I finally felt brave enough to take Bishop's hand in my own.

"Let's say I say yes."

Leaves bristled under our feet on the pathway. I had no follow-up, so I let the words air out in the dark, like wet laundry in need of drying.

"Let's say you do, then."

We found a picnic table just off the edge of a grove of trees, nestled away between some fallen branches from the last hurricane and a boundary of a path that appeared abandoned that time of day. Bishop pulled another cigarette from the carton in his pocket, and I hopped up on the tabletop, placing my backpack on the seat beside me. A bird called from somewhere in the distance, a tiny melody playing an accompaniment to the whisper of the naked trees.

"You realize that's your second cigarette in fifteen minutes?"

Bishop shook his head, lighting the smoke with a grin creeping across his face. I tilted my head sideways and stared at him, the sun fading out around us, the outline of the moon visible in the cotton candy sky. He was doing an awful lot of chain-smoking for someone who wasn't feeling anxious.

"Don't change the subject." He boosted himself up on the tabletop next to me, handing over the cigarette again in a comfortable, back and forth fashion. I breathed the warm smoke in with a nose full of autumn air, a tornado forming in my lungs.

"Fine—I'll be you and be forward and blunt about this whole ordeal." Bishop smiled at me, amused. "You're attractive, I like you, I'm glad Gemma's out of the picture."

"Well, that's certainly one way of putting things."

I took another short pull on the smoke before handing it back, coils of vapor worming their way into circulation.

"How would you have put things then?" I asked the question with a lighthearted tone and leave him to think for a moment as he smokes. His words were not what I expected.

"You're attractive, I like you, I'm glad Gemma's out of the picture."

Then he took my chin in his hand, pulled me toward him, and we kissed again underneath the watchful eyes of the empty forest.

I never knew anyone to ride their motorcycle far into the fall, but Bishop was a purist, and he claimed he would always wait until the last possible day to put it away until spring. There was no bone in my body that wanted to get on the bike with him, not a single iota of one, but I loved the way he looked when he rode, and I couldn't resist the things his helmet did to his hair. He always had a way of running his hands through the mop and making the pieces stand up in exactly the most perfect and alluring way. It was sexy, in a disheveled sort of fashion.

The evening we spent in the park, Bishop hadn't taken his bike to class but rather a plain black Kia Rio hatch. I hadn't even thought about the logistics of winter transportation, which was amusing considering the season in the province lasted for what felt like half the year. On top of that, it was closing in quickly, a snowfall soon on the breeze once the frost began gathering.

But the relevance of that started much earlier, only to be discerned later.

It was entirely dark by the time Bishop and I unraveled from each other, stars spotting the nighttime sky to keep the moon company up in the universe. It was as if time had both slowed and passed alarmingly, a haze of confusion wrapped around our lips and seeping into the preoccupation of our brains.

"Hell, Tee," Bishop whispered the words into my neck, hands pressing my own down flat on the wooden surface of the table. "I wish I would have done this earlier."

"I wish you would have too. But I can't help but think perhaps it would have been too soon. At least this way I feel less like I've destroyed your relationship, instead of being the girl who allowed it to dissolve organically." I smiled into the lapel of his jacket as he nibbled at my collarbone, lips trailing a gentle mark along the spot he was searching for. My hands tucked into the empty, exposed skin of his lower back, nails tracing the texture.

"Organically. Hmmm. That's an interesting way to word it." Bishop pulled my earlobe between his teeth and gave it a tug, forcing my fingers to dig into his sides.

I growled a deep and throaty sound that escaped me before I could even begin to control it.

"We could go back to my place if you want?"

Bishop propped himself upright, brushing my hair from both our faces.

"I'm forcing myself to say no, Tee. We should take things easy for just a little bit. Gemma knows too many people around here, and I don't want you caught in our drama."

"What kind of drama are we looking at?" My hands slid to his own, and he gently pulled me toward him, my feet touching the gravel path.

"Not drama you want." Bishop handed me my bag before throwing his over his shoulder. "Gemma's dad works for the school."

"Our school? Why doesn't she go here then?"

We began walking back toward the gates, an owl hunting for mice swooping between the branches of the tall trees. Sounds seemed louder in the night, each gust of wind and the symphony of branches tapping against each other like a series of mini explosions in the quiet of early November.

"Got a full scholarship to the pre-law program at Davis. Since Fischer is kind of lacking in the legal department, she opted to go elsewhere."

I nodded into the blackness, rasping my shoulder against Bishop's arm. We walked back to the Fischer parking lot in silence, where he stopped next to the Kia.

"No bike today?"

"Try to avoid riding in the dark when I can. Have had too many close calls in the city to risk it when I can avoid it. Thursdays, I drive the car since I'm usually late. Pick up my groceries and that sort of thing."

"So responsible."

Bishop laughed and pulled me to his chest, burying his face in my hair. I could smell his aftershave again, combined with the general scent of him, and I greedily sucked it in and hoped my own clothes would absorb some for later. If I couldn't have him in bed with me, I at least wanted to feel a little bit like he was still around. My body ached at the thought. There was a tangible pain at our separation.

"Hop in. I'll drive you home."

"I live three minutes down the road, Bishop."

"Just get in."

So, I did.

Bishop turned the key in the ignition and flicked the heat on low, the car encased in a chill from sitting empty all day long. As he backed out of the parking spot our eyes met, and I could feel a crimson flush working its way up my face, a tingling heat crossing through my lips and down to my thighs.

It itched my nerves and massaged my veins in a storm of greed and desire.

In no time at all we were at my place, the car idling out front as I stared up at the case of stairs leading me away.

"You sure you don't want to come up?"

"It's nothing to do with not wanting to, Tee."

"I know. I'm playing. Have a good weekend."

I opened the car door, dome light blazing the interior into brightness.

"I have to move the rest of Gemma's stuff home, and I've got an English Lit paper due Monday. But I'll text you, alright?" Bishop had a rosy glow, either an embarrassed flush or an indicator of his hormones.

"Okay." I climbed out of the Kia, letting in the cold. "Thanks for the distraction."

"I think we both needed one."

I nodded and shut the door, closing Bishop in the machine to travel back through the narrow streets to his own home. Tucking my scarf out of my way, I slung my bag over my shoulder, heading for the door. I couldn't wipe the stupid grin off my face.

"Tee!"

I whipped around, Bishop half hanging out the passenger side window of the car.

"What, you fool?" I giggled at the visual of his body contorted over the seats and console.

"Are you my girlfriend now?"

I laughed. And not a tiny, muffled laugh, but an unabashed one that shook out all my tension.

Thursdays became our days. There was something celebratory about the end of the school week, every weekend being a long one, and the development of a quiet relationship in the throes of another being dissolved. Gradually my worry about Gemma waned, faster than I anticipated but not without retaining issues. I felt invincible with Bishop.

Then it all fell apart—on a Thursday. I had a paper due for Sociology.

I got the assignment done just in time, crashing my way into Wyatt's class approximately three seconds before he started lecturing. Dropping my papers into the collection basket just as he picked it up from the requisite drop off spot by the classroom door, Professor Wyatt gave me an audible sigh, clearly hoping he was going to be able to rain on someone's parade.

Not me and not today.

I took my seat—back row, left corner—and pulled my phone out from my pocket as I set my binder down on my desk.

Dinner?

I'm in Soc

After?

I tried to think about what I might have in my cupboards that I could make. I've always been an absolutely horrendous cook, but the logic of this rivals my desire to impress Bishop.

Spaghetti?

They don't serve that at CL

I'm cooking

Fancy girl. I'm in.

If I could remember how to make the damn stuff, we would be golden.

For the sake of explanation, I didn't do a whole lot of properly feeding myself that year, lunches coming from an after-thought purchase of a meal card for campus and breakfast being a non-existent word in my vocabulary. Dinner was always dicey. Dinner with Bishop was a practical impossibility.

But I tried.

We had a cyclical and predictably timed relationship, meeting again after our respective Thursday evening classes by the doors to Cedar Lounge. Bishop had a cigarette hanging from his mouth, lit this time, a pair of fingerless wool gloves permitting him to smoke and maintain dexterity.

"Hi, Tee."

He kissed me long and slow, his lips cold and smoky but thick with longing. The outdoor path lights leading to Cedar Lounge hummed an insect-like buzz in the cold, the doors firmly shut and heat steaming the windows of the bar. A few students were having a late meal, but otherwise, the place was nearly empty. Lance polished glasses behind the counter and could be spotted from the far window if someone were looking.

I wasn't.

"Bish!" A voice called, nearby and familiar. "Remove your lips from your girlfriend—I've got your phone."

Michael Harvey, an acquaintance of Bishops from English Lit.

I launched myself away from Bishop's face as fast as I could, but it wasn't fast enough.

"Whoa, Talia? You're not Gemma." Michael handed Bishop his phone with hardly a glance,

Shawna/Tessa smirking at his side. "Girl, what is going on here?"

I wiped at my lips as if I could rub off the evidence, even though Michael had seen it with his own eyes.

"Gemma and I split a bit back, Mike."

The overhead lights continued their electric melody, but we were silent, waiting for one another to break.

"So, you scooped in and picked this up? You go, Tee. Getting in there before I could entice him to switch teams. Sneaky."

"I don't think that's how sexual orientation works, you know." Bishop was lost and starting to ramble.

"Um, well," I tried to think up something as inconspicuous as possible, but fell flat.

"Talia and I are studying for finals." Bishop tried his hardest to think up something in the moment, but it was absolutely no use. Michael knew what was going on. The trouble now was going to be controlling his big mouth.

"Oh please, honey. You do you. Guess that's going to make Wyatt's class awfully awkward for you though, won't it Tee?"

"What do you mean?" I was confused for about five seconds until I managed to piece together exactly what was going on.

Shawna/Tessa shifted back and forth on her four-inch heeled boots while she waited for me to smarten up.

"Oh shit, Wyatt is Gemma's father?"

Bishop did a partial nod, telling me everything I needed to know.

"It never really came up, Talia. I didn't think it was a big deal."

My hands started shaking, and my mind moved at a million miles per second. I tried to rationalize all my thoughts as they came. *What is the actual issue with Professor Wyatt being the father of Bishop's ex? The semester was almost over anyway.*

"Well, except that Wyatt is the prof for all the mandatory Sociology courses. And since Tee is a Soc major …" Michael trailed off, Bishop glowering at him.

"Jesus, Mike. Fuck us before we even get started."

"I think you guys started long before I came in here. You've been making eyes at each other for months. Frankly, I'm glad you got rid of Gemma. Talia's a better, albeit more complicated, choice."

I laughed, both nervously and awkwardly.

"Wyatt doesn't have to know. Gemma doesn't have to know." Bishop ran through the ideas as fast as he could, syllables tripping out of his mouth.

"Bish, how big do you think this damn town is? And I just processed Talia's teaching assistant application from back during frosh week. She's in for next year." Michael flashed me one of his signature smiles.

"I'm in?" I was floored. "I forgot I even put my name forward. They never pick first years. My marks aren't even available."

"Wyatt requested you. Turns out you have the highest mark anyone's ever received in his class."

Bishop stared me down, the last remaining bits of his cigarette burning out in his fingers, forgotten.

"Shit."

I tried not to think about the teaching assistant position for as long as I could possibly delay, winding myself up in walks with Bishop and classes and library sessions with my best friend, Mandy. I'd been told that November has a tendency to pass quickly in university, class sizes dropping from people deciding not to return and the bombardment of due dates stapling all the days of the week together. I didn't think about it until a week later, when Bishop stood outside the door of Wyatt's class, waiting for me to take our traditional Thursday excursion.

I didn't know he was there, but he must have come looking for me when I didn't show up outside of our meeting spot at the rocks by Cedar Lounge. It was a sweet gesture, picking me up from class, but I don't think he considered the repercussions of his actions.

Professor Wyatt had pulled me aside after class to confirm that he had selected me for the opening next year. He clarified for me that teaching assistant positions were very lucrative at the university, often filled a year in advance to allow for students to plan their course loads around the work. When he spoke to me, he didn't seem to be aware in any way that I was the reason for his daughter's move back home or the falling apart of a wedding that was in the planning stages.

Or maybe he was trying to kill me with kindness.

"So, the long and the short of it is you'll be marking my assignments, quizzes, exams, and doing some research on the side. I'm hoping you can periodically make yourself available for this class, which will be held at the same time slot next year, as well as office hours once a week."

Wyatt explained the details slowly, much in the same way he lectured.

"That shouldn't be an issue."

"Of course, you'll be paid a set rate that we can put toward your tuition for the following semester if you wish. I don't have that information on me, but I can get hold of it for you in the next few weeks."

"That would be lovely, thank you." I really was thankful. I had received an entrance scholarship for the majority of my first year, but the onset of worry hadn't avoided me with respect as to how I was planning on paying the rest of my way.

"I'll let you get on with your evening. I'm pleased to hear you accept, Miss Anderson." Professor Wyatt gathered his briefcase, buttoning his aged tweed jacket as he prepared to exit. "I'll see you next class. I look forward to working with you."

You wouldn't be looking forward to it if you knew.

He walked through the threshold of the door, turning to his left. Then I heard the words, and I expected the world to implode on itself right then and there.

"Ah, Bishop Gale. To what do I owe the honor?" There was a hint of sarcasm in the voice if I could infer sarcasm on someone's tone that I was barely familiar with.

"I'm here for Talia." The words were simple, but they slowly crushed Professor Wyatt's face into a contemptuous sneer as he peered back at me.

"You know each other?"

I hoisted my bag on my back, keeping my sightline clear with the door but not moving from my spot next to the desk at the front of the room. Then I froze.

"Bishop, if you do anything to screw up Gemma's grades in her first year of pre-law, there's going to be hell to pay. You need to apologize to her, and our family needs to move on. Whatever you did …   are doing," he glared at me as if I were poisonous. "It needs to end. Don't screw this up for everyone."

And with those words, Wyatt brushed past Bishop while I stood, frozen, my mouth unable to shut and my mind incapable of processing what had just happened.

"What the fuck, Bishop?"

"I'm sorry, Tee! I wasn't thinking. I swear." He charged into the classroom and took me in his arms, holding me close enough to hear his heart thumping through the fabric of his jacket.

"He won't do anything to your job, he's not the type."

"I need that position to pay for next year's tuition. I sure as hell hope not." The words left my mouth and were absorbed by Bishop's chest where I mumbled them. He ran his hands through the ends of my hair, tugging gently and bringing my face toward his.

"I'll figure it out."

I thought on Professor Wyatt's words for a moment, trying to regulate my breathing.

"What do you have to apologize for?"

Bishop sighed deeply and let me go.

"Wyatt thinks I just have cold feet about the wedding."

"So, he doesn't know Gemma's been the one screwing around?"

"His perfect daughter? Of course not, Talia. Why would I ever tell him something like that?"

The building was quiet around us, classes empty for the evening and students gone off to their dorms or to the Cedar Lounge for whatever party was being held that night.

"Does he think I'm just some girl you're sleeping with?"

"I don't know what he thinks, Tee, but it certainly isn't the truth of the situation."

This made me feel a little bit better about the entire set of circumstances. But still, I stood in front of Bishop, unsure of what to say in response. Then I noticed the helmet in his hand.

"Brought your bike tonight? But it's Thursday?"

"I thought I could take you for a ride."

Panic rose in my chest, heart palpitating.

"I'm not so sure about that."

Bishop grinned at me, taking my hand to lead me from the classroom.

"Can we at least get out of here then? I'll ride the bike, and you can run behind me if that's what you'd prefer."

I punched him in the arm for that comment, squeezing our bodies close together between the spaces of the desk rows. Flicking off the light at the door, Bishop pressed me against the wall, arms trapping my body with him.

"I've got another helmet on the bike. Please, Tee?" His lips drew ever closer, and I did my best to resist. "Please?"

I leaned toward him, and he leaned back, replacing the inch between us.

"I don't think so." I just couldn't get on that bike.

"That's unfortunate," he whispered into the tiny air between us. "I thought maybe in return

I'd give you a little incentive." Bishop slowly licked my bottom lip, chest pressing against my own as my backpack smashed into the wall behind me. I saw little bits of stars as my mind began to wander. Tucking my fingers in his own, Bishop squeezed my hands, trailing his mouth down my jawline, stopping at the bundle of scarf I was wearing at the time. Then he abruptly pulled away.

"Don't."

I breathed out the word before I even realized I was doing it.

"Get on the bike then." He groaned the words out, softly, right into my ear.

"Fine. Give me the helmet. Just don't stop."

He stopped.

He promised me that later he wouldn't, but after all, we were in the classroom used by his ex-girlfriend's father. There was absolutely nothing to wind me up or turn me on with respect to that setting, and so I didn't hold anything against Bishop except myself.

We walked to the parking lot under a clear blanket of Prussian blue and specks of twinkling ivory, a milky full moon lighting the path past Cedar Lounge. The campus was mostly empty, a few students traversing the pebbled paths, but like so many other Thursday nights, there were other pre-occupations for people our age rather than the ones Bishop and I were managing.

Bishop handed me a helmet and fitted the strapping to my head as I tried my hardest not to look anxious. I could feel my legs shaking as he took the seat in front of me, turning on the motorcycle with a low and rumbling growl. The vibrations shook from my thighs up through my ribs to my heart, rippling sensations I hadn't ever felt through the context of my body. I could feel the mechanical power, but I also could sense Bishop close between my legs and this gave me a whole other set of tactile pleasures.

"You ready?" He called the words over top of the noise of the bike, giving my knee a squeeze. I don't think I responded, but he didn't wait for my words anyway, easing out of the spot between the marked yellow lines. We were moving, and I held my breath, waiting for the impact of immediately hitting the pavement.

We didn't.

I can't come up with a practical enough descriptor to illustrate the way riding on the back of Bishop's bike made me feel. There was something freeing about the open city road and the lack of protective doors. I felt dangerous, untouchable, and uninhibited. And in that second, I understood what a change of pace

Thursday nights must have been for Bishop over the past few weeks.

Gradually, my death grip on Bishop loosened, and in a minute and a half, we arrived at my place. In ninety seconds my opinion of motorcycles had done a complete one-eighty. By the time we parked on the street in front of my flat, I was barely hanging on at all. I was exhilarated.

"You survived," Bishop smiled, pulling the helmet off me. My blonde hair was crushed against my head, tangled up from the wind and knotted like I'd spent the day at the beach.

"That wasn't even close to as bad as I expected."

"Good," Bishop confirmed. "I kind of figured that when we turned the corner and you finally breathed." He tugged off his own helmet, revealing his face and disheveled spikes.

"You could feel all that?"

"Hard not to feel someone trying to crush your ribcage. You've got quite a grip on you."

I glowed red with embarrassment as Bishop headed up the steps, leaving me trailing behind. Bounding behind him, I strung my book-bag onto my arm, pulling out my keys to let us both in. The door was barely unlocked before he had thrust me into the same position we were in not all that long before, the deepness of the night making a veritable blanket around our exchange.

I dropped my bag onto the entryway mat, Bishop locking on to my lips and crashing through the door without so much as a sideways glance. I kicked my shoes out of the way as I wrapped my hands around the back of his neck, nails running over the nape and getting caught on the tag of his sweater.

"I told you I wouldn't stop." He breathed the words out in a harried rush.

"This time, don't make me get on a motorcycle in the middle, please." Bishop smiled into my lips as he kissed them, tongue licking at the corners of my mouth until I finally let him in.

He knew the way to the bedroom with his eyes closed, but he dragged out our spontaneity instead of heading right for the action we both were desperate for.

Placing the helmet on the dining room table, Bishop never let me go, one hand on my face and the other making it to my hip then up the back of my shirt. His fingers were chilled from the autumn wind blowing over top of them on the bike, the cool temperature at odds with the warmth of my skin. His touch made me shiver, and he responded to the reaction by slipping his other hand up my thigh and lifting me onto the maple surface.

"Tell me when you want me to stop."

Never. Never, ever stop making me feel this way.

Bishop sank his teeth into my neck, biting down hard and making my throat tighten. I whined a carnal sound from between my lips, and my hands instinctively grasped the hem of his shirt and pulled it up over his head. He was caged in his own clothing before he wrestled himself free, losing the clothing to the abyss of the floor. Exposed, he stood there in the dark, and I could see the outline of a tattoo on his hip as he sank down onto me again.

Bishop toyed with the rim of my shirt for a few seconds before he gathered enough courage to undress me, exposing my chest in a red lace bra I had never worn for any other occasion. There were no words exchanged, no sharp inhale or examination, just a second of hesitation before his hands found the clasp on my back and brought it free in one quick motion.

I sighed as Bishop's lips found their way down over me, and I tugged at the errant pieces of his hair as his mouth worked my body.

My fingers fumbled with his belt in the blackness, the leather smooth on my prints as I swiped the end from the buckle.

"Tee," he mouthed.

"Hmmm?"

"This okay?"

I didn't want to tell him that everything was okay, I wanted to show him. And so, instead of simply saying yes, I propped my hips on the edge of the dining room table and slipped him delicately out of his jeans. Another tattoo snaked up his leg—something botanical. He was good at hiding them.

Or maybe I was just good at hunting them down.

Maybe there's another under what's left of his clothes.

I dared myself to find it.

It became immediately clear that Bishop and I were made for each other—but he was one kiss away from killing me. I didn't think my heart could beat any faster, that my breath could catch in my throat any more without asphyxiating me. Every inch of my body groaned and tingled and sparked and begged for Bishop; desperate. I was desperate and aching for him, and I had no words to explain because my brain was no longer in my head.

Bishop's six-foot frame encompassed my smaller one the second I pulled off my jeans. He grabbed me by my thighs and had me straddle him while he walked to the bedroom, nosing my neck all the way. By the light of the moon, he placed me down on the comforter, easing himself on top of me.

"Talia?"

His voice was low and sounded like it belonged to someone else.

"Say my name again." I wanted to swallow his voice, digest it, make it a part of me to have whenever I wanted.

"Oh, you like the bedroom voice?"

I chuckled, sinking myself farther underneath him. Pulling myself up to reach him, I fastened my lips to his exposed shoulder and mumbled a response.

"Very much so."

"Hmmm," Bishop groaned into my ear, latching on to my neck again and dislodging my own mouth. I could feel his hips pressing against me, hard and ready, and I was barely able to control myself. My fingers pressed into the flesh of his thighs and tempted him toward me, but he resisted, keeping his casual pace.

"Talia. We have all night."

I didn't want to wait.

"Then we can do it twice."

Bishop's fingers trailed up my side and across my chest, and I could tell he was smiling.

"When I'm done with you, you won't have enough energy to go again."

I sucked in my breath, half because of what he was saying and half because of the way he sounded when he said it.

"Maybe I have plans for you too," I retorted, slipping my hand from his thigh to take him in it.

Bishop bit his lip, and I watched his expression change with each drag of my fingers, every change of pressure. I was soon met with his own hands, finding their way around me with a familiar adeptness. It only took seconds, my first one, but I had no time for repose as the second built up in the space between my thighs.

"Not yet, not yet." Bishop removed his hand and placed it on top of my own. "Please, dear God, don't change your mind now."

I didn't respond with my words. Instead, I guided him into me. He moved slowly, savoring the seconds and the sensation, and I could do nothing about the throaty, audible groan that escaped. Bishop's hips met my own, deep and intense, and I felt myself tense around him, squeezing, capsizing his attempt to last longer.

We started moving together, delicately at first, then hard and rushed and frantic as if we had limited time and a schedule to keep. Bishop took hold of my headboard in one hand and a grasp of my hair in the other, watching me through narrowed eyes. He was rough and sensual and animalistic and entirely consuming.

"Soon, Tee. So soon."

Between twisted sheets, clenched fingers, and shuddered breaths, I let him have all of me, over and over again until neither of us could handle any more.

Bishop was right after all. I didn't have the energy for another round, instead choosing to wrap myself in the blankets and curl up next to him, watching the moon out of the bedroom window. It doesn't go anywhere, but I keep my eye on it, just in case it falls out of the sky in disbelief.

"I need water." Bishop's voice crackled, dry and parched with activity. "You want anything?"

I stretched out my toes under the blankets.

"I'm good. Very good."

The words have sleep dripping from them, a hand grazing my hair before he slips out of bed and disappears into the shadows of the hallway. I unfold myself in the middle of the bed, taking inventory of the sensations in my body. My thighs whined with use, I could feel the tiny bruises forming on my neck and shoulders, and my muscles hummed with satisfaction. A few deep breaths filled me and then there was a tiny light in the dark.

My phone.

I reached across the bed, the device squashed in between discarded pillows. The backlight was still lit, and I realized once I picked it up that it was Bishop's phone, not mine, a conversation open on the screen.

Gemma's name blazed along the top.

When are you going to come home?

I don't know, Gem. Dad says he met the girl you've been fucking around on me with. That blonde from the Halloween party? Dressed as a cop? Really?

She's sweet. Hurry up and screw her so we can get on with our lives. Dad picked her as his TA. Think she's going to pick you over a job?

I don't know. Maybe?

Then what? You disappear? Good luck, Bee.

"Talia?"

I dropped the phone on the covers, a hairpin trigger response.

"Care to explain this?" My fingertips went numb with the amount of rage I was feeling.

"Why do you have my phone?"

Bishop doesn't move from the doorway, a mug of water in his left hand. He's stark naked, which is distracting of its own accord, but at the moment I'm more occupied looking at the hurt and anger written across his face. Then there's a glimmer of something else—something that he knows means he's caught.

"It was in the bed. Thought it was mine. Better question … what's going on with you and Gemma? And don't lie to me, I already know you're a shit liar."

Bishop took a sip from the cup and crossed the room to sit on the edge of the bed.

"It's not what you think. Gemma isn't taking the whole break up thing very well. She seems to think I've just gotten a little distracted."

"Oh, and why would she think that?"

There was a period of contemplation, hesitation.

"I told her that."

"Get the fuck out." My voice wavered, but I was serious. In that second, he needed to go. I didn't want to hear his side of the story, the shock and the hormones still cruising through my body. There was no rational thought, and Bishop knew it.

"Talia, let me explain."

"You have thirty seconds. And put some goddamn pants on."

Bishop must have known I was deadly serious because he actually listened to me when

I told him to put on some pants. He sat his mug down on the night table, a little blue cup with a gold dipped handle I had purchased as a set of four from the grocery store back when I first moved in, and went back out to the living room to retrieve all his clothing before returning. I figured that it probably would be hypocritical of me to not also follow my own request, so I dug out whatever was in front of my closet and threw it on. Sheets and blankets were dropped haphazardly onto the bed, a puddle of fabric gathering on the mattress.

"Talia, please."

I flicked on all the lights I came across, trying to drown out the darkness that had just encompassed us.

"Your thirty seconds starts now, Bishop." I wasn't about to let him forget that my actions were all for a greater purpose.

"Fuck, okay." He ran a hand over his face, following me in my rampage around the apartment. "It's like I said, Gemma is taking this poorly, and I'm trying not to make things awkward for her or you with your job offer and all. Gemma's dad has a lot of pull around the school. I kind of got myself into a mess."

"No shit, eh?" I whipped around, throwing a discarded decorative pillow back on the bed before stomping into the living room. The remnants of my outfit from earlier in the day were scattered along the floor.

"Look, why don't you ask the questions and I'll give the answers. You'll probably get what you need that way."

I'll give it to him, it's a good plan, and I can't poke any holes in it.

"Fine. Question one… are you still screwing Gemma?"

Bishop sighed, putting his hands on my shoulders in a futile attempt to hold me still from my buzzing about.

"No. Really, Tee. I'm not. She moved back home."

"Because she was cheating on you or because you got cold feet about the wedding?" A pause, a telltale one, gave me the information I never knew I was going to need. "Shit, Bishop. Really?"

"No, no, no," he tried to cover up and correct the foundation he just put down. "It's a little bit of both. And a little bit extra."

"Extra?"

"I met you, Talia. I really do like you. But I have a very real worry that I'm going to mess up your TA thing with Wyatt. And I know you need that. It concerns me."

I studied his face, looking for the lie, the deceit, the attempt to get out of the conversation as quickly as possible, but I found nothing but the truth.

"Why don't you leave that worry up to me since it's my money and my life? It's only been a few weeks, and you're already thinking about how you're going to ruin my life?"

My brain was telling me to shut the hell up, but my mouth just wouldn't listen. I scooped up the dregs of my clothes and dumped them in a clump on my laundry hamper by the bathroom.

"Talia, don't be like this about it. You know as well as I do that it's been a few weeks in the works for a long time. And we have so many months ahead of us."

I sighed, flopping down on the couch now that I had nothing left to flutter over.

"Just … tell her it's over. I'll work on Wyatt, and you work on Gemma, and we can figure all this out, okay?"

Bishop took a seat beside me and kissed my tangled mess of hair.

"I'm sorry I didn't tell you about this sooner."

"It's only been a few weeks," I recycled the words. "There's only been so much time to figure out the rest of our lives."

Bishop laughed, and I knew, in that moment, that everything was going to be alright if I could just slow down and take things with a more logical approach.

"How are you feeling, anyway?" The question was low and safe, and the way Bishop mouthed the letters told me that he was truly looking for a legitimate answer, one that I didn't filter.

"Amazing. Other than the part where I freaked out. I feel bad about that. Can I blame hormones? I've just had a rush of those, and they don't exactly make me logical."

"Does that mean I'm safe to see if you want to go again?" Bishop crawled over top of me, my back adjusting to the press against the cushions of the couch as he pushed my shoulders down. I did a mental check of my body, trying to ascertain if I would be up for another round of what we had earlier. He sensed my hesitation. "I'll be nicer this time, I promise."

"You were plenty nice last time, we just got a little rougher than I expected for our first time. Usually, the first time with someone new is awkward and tentative. The first time for us was—"

"Explosive?"

I got an amusing visual and couldn't help the grunt that popped out of my throat.

"That's certainly one way to describe it. I mean, not the one I was thinking, but definitely an accurate depiction."

Bishop kissed me once, deeply, then a second time but quickly.

"So, is that a yes or a no, then?"

"We both just got dressed, Bish."

"Perfect, then I can undress you all over again." He slipped his hands up the front of my shirt, caressing my braless chest, and bringing the fabric up to expose my stomach. His lips traced tiny circles on my skin as his hands tugged down the waistband of my pants.

"Wait, one more question."

"Hmmm." Bishop hummed into my hip bone, licking a line from one side to the other.

"What do you think? Should I pick you or the job?"

Bishop groaned, looking up at me from his position between my legs.

"Can a job get you off like I can?"

I think on the question for a second as he pinched my side and I squealed, combing my fingers through his hair and pulling at the ends.

"Depends on the job."

The final Thursday of November was abnormally cold, the temperature dropping lower than seasonally average. The first light snowfall began while I was in Professor Wyatt's class, and now that I think back on it, I should have taken it as an omen for something. The only thing I understood of it was that it meant I needed to find my winter coat sooner than I anticipated.

The large, ivory flakes glided past the glass of the window, lit from outside by the campus streetlights, and projected tiny dark spots on the walls. There were only ten minutes left in the class when the weather began, and being the premiere of the season, it attracted an awful lot of attention from a room of disinterested sociology students. Wyatt kept talking as if nothing was happening. Really, nothing was.

Bits of sky are falling. No big deal.

"Alright, chapter fourteen next week and then we're done for the semester. I'll be giving out the examination outline on Tuesday and answering any questions you may have other than the ones on specific content. Please be careful traveling home this evening as the snow has started." He capped his marker and set it down on the tray by the whiteboard. "Talia, a word, please. Have a good weekend, everyone."

It must have taken under thirty seconds for the entire class to vacate the premises, while I remained at my back-row desk until my peers all escaped.

"Miss Anderson?"

"Yes?"

"I understand you are still interested in the teaching assistant position?" Professor Wyatt picked up a small group of file folders and walked to the desk in front of me, setting his things on it while he stood over me.

"Yes, thank you. Were you able to get me those details that you mentioned the other week?"

"Not so fast, Miss Anderson. There's something else we need to discuss." I gave him a quizzical look, unsure of exactly what he meant. He filled in the gaps for me.

"Bishop Gale."

"What about him?" I was able to predict where exactly the conversation was heading, but I didn't want to give away my position so early in the interrogation. I had learned in my intro psychology class that it was best in these situations to let the other side begin the negotiation.

"I don't want any distractions during your appointment. I'm familiar with Mister Gale, and unfortunately, I know he would be one."

Full stop.

"With respect, Professor, but I am also familiar with Bishop, and I'm certain I can manage all of my responsibilities even with his existence." I could hear a tone edging my voice as Professor Wyatt sighed.

"You may know Mister Gale used to date my daughter, Gemma?"

"I am vaguely aware of the fact, sir."

"Are you also vaguely aware of the circumstances surrounding their current situation?" He took my words and twisted them around, a soupy and sarcastic tone housed inside.

"I've heard about a potential wedding," I began, but Wyatt cut me off.

"There will be a wedding, Miss Anderson. Now, whatever is going on between you and Bishop needs to very quickly come to an end. I'll give you until Christmas break to sort out your little affair. If you can't sort it out, I can't let you have the position. It's too lucrative to give away to a student who is going to spend all her time running around."

I'm sure that my jaw hit the floor as he made his points, the snow no longer my only distraction from the starkness of the classroom.

"Are you giving me an ultimatum?" I voiced the question slowly as if I didn't believe the words I was asking.

Wyatt collected his folders; a red one, two blue, and a goldenrod.

"I'm giving you a choice. You can put my daughter's life back together, or you can have your own fall apart."

I couldn't help myself. There was a ball of fire in my stomach that burned to tell Wyatt the absolute truth about his daughter, and because I felt threatened and wanted to get the upper hand, I did.

"You know your daughter's been screwing some guy from her Econ class in the frat down the road from your house?"

Wyatt laughed.

"Is that what your new boyfriend told you?" He didn't seem at all concerned with my assertion. "Gemma's cousin Jonathan is in the fraternity. Transferred in to Davis this year. I understand they've been spending some time together. Of course, since they're cousins that would be spending time together of a non-sexual nature."

I couldn't think of anything to say back, so I was struck into silence.

"Think about what I said, Talia. You can let me know after exams."

Professor Wyatt sauntered out of the class, head held high, back straight. I heard him mention a muffled greeting to Bishop who stood outside the door, obviously not getting the hint about the last time he had met me directly after class.

I didn't get up from my chair.

"What was that about?"

I could feel the tears welling up in my eyes, my face turning red from the frustration I had just experienced. But I got through telling Bishop about the whole encounter before I finally let myself cry a single tear, the salt water running a strip down my cheek.

"He knows about us. He says it's you or the job. I just ... I can't believe we even had that conversation."

Bishop kissed the top of my forehead.

"I'm going to go have a chat with Gemma. This needs to stop, Talia. Please don't worry yet, I'll try and get things sorted out."

"Really? You'd do that?"

"Why not? I'll come by after, okay?"

I nodded, itching at the leftover tears on my face.

"Did you bring the Kia? It's snowing."

"No, but I'll be careful. Wasn't supposed to start snowing today. Not sticking on the ground anyway. I'll pick up the Kia before I come back in case we want to go out."

I smiled as much as I could, and Bishop took my hand, pulling me up from my seat.

"Come on. Walk with me to the parking lot. I'll text Gemma and see if she'll meet me at my place. Get everything over with all at once, and we won't have to explain why I'm showing up at her place."

"Good plan."

I had to admit, it sounded bulletproof. I was hoping that if Bishop spoke with Gemma then we could put an end to this whole issue. But part of me still worried about the financial aspect of my next year at Fischer. Would I be able to find another job or another appointment as a teaching assistant in time?

The air was arctic, but the wind was still, and Bishop was right in that the snow wasn't gathering on the road but turning into nothing as it hit the blacktop. The grass, or what was left of it, had a tiny crusting of white that crunched under my boots when I ventured off the path. I could imagine there were stars up in the black of the sky, but it was interrupted by tumbling pieces of encapsulated water.

Cedar Lounge was empty.

It was another sign, but I didn't know it.

Bishop didn't come back, and the sky kept falling, tiny pieces of outer space finding a home on our soil.

A thick and inky black consumed the atmosphere, grey with fog patches that covered the moon and bit away at the midnight air. Its very existence was casually interrupted by flakes of snow, sparkling and spattering the canvas of night. I watched it all live outside of my bedroom window, hoping for the moment I would hear from Bishop, and he would tell me everything was going to be alright. To keep myself occupied, I wrapped myself in the sheets of my bed and stared into the outdoors, waiting for an answer.

Hours passed that way.

I read a book, but I couldn't tell you what it was about.

I messaged Mandy.

I tried to sleep, but I was restless, and so I finally texted Bishop.

You coming back?

A half hour later, after chronic radio silence:

Bishop?
Are things okay with Gemma?

I felt a little worried, as anyone would have given my circumstances, but mostly I had a nibbling feeling on my insides that maybe things weren't exactly as they seemed. Nothing could shake for me the idea that maybe Professor Wyatt had also given Bishop an ultimatum, one that he couldn't refuse.

I'm going to bed - if you come back, you know where the spare key is.

But I wasn't going to bed. I mean, the truth was I was in it already, but there was no way I was going to sleep. As soon as I closed my eyes, pictures started floating around my head of Bishop and Gemma together again, and for the life of me, I couldn't make them go away. The depictions kept me up well past three in the morning, and I knew at that point Bishop wasn't going to be returning to see me. He was taking care of something, working out a detail I didn't need to be part of, despite that I was at least half of the problem he was incurring in the first place.

Suspicion rose in my throat like bile, a sick, acidic feeling that fed on my insides and my anxiety as if it were something to be digested. Eventually, it dissipated enough for me to fall asleep, but it was an agitated one, unsteady and transient.

Morning arrived. He didn't come back.

Not that night, not that weekend. I texted him half a dozen times, called him at least that many, but I never received a response. No cursory voicemail to say he was staying with Gemma or brief message to let me know Wyatt had gotten under his skin enough to serve as a premise for abandonment. I must have checked my phone every two minutes until Monday, but nothing ever came.

I was alone.

Did something happen with Gemma?

The answer was an obvious and resounding yes, but I wanted Bishop to tell me that on his own.

Then, Sunday evening, I started to feel desperate. Amidst the crackling grass, I walked to Bishop's place on North Street, a good fifteen blocks from my own. But he was worth it. An answer would be worth it too.

The evening was cotton candy; pink and blue swirls twisted their way through the sky, perching on the roofs of buildings and the tops of trees like colored floss. My ivory scarf made for a warm, knitted hood to protect my face and neck from the pending December chill, while my hands remained exposed. I didn't like gloves. I still don't.

I crossed Leeds Street to North, no traffic coming either way, an empty night with a demure allure. Three houses down from my location I could see Bishop's little yellow house. No motorcycle in the driveway, but a Kia sitting on the asphalt, unmoved in what appeared to be days. I knocked on the door over and over, but the curtains were drawn, and the windows were dark.

He wasn't there.

Mashing some snow between my fingers, I built a little, tiny snowball and threw it at his front picture window. It landed with a wet and lazy thop, then the city around me was still again.

The thought crossed my mind to go to Gemma's, but I didn't think that Professor Wyatt would approve of me showing up randomly on a Sunday. On top of that, he was trying to convince me to stay away from Bishop, not follow some sparsely populated breadcrumbs to try and track him down.

I stuffed my hands in the pockets of my coat, fingers turning red from the cold and the droplets of the leftover snowball. They touched the smooth edge of my phone, and I couldn't help myself but to pull it out and check it again.

Still nothing.

I'm at your place - you around?

I don't know why I bothered sending a message. He hadn't answered any of my other ones, so my expectation that he might finally start to respond was practically unfounded. After pacing in front of the house for another five minutes, I finally went home.

Sunday grew and shrunk in importance without Bishop's presence and slowly dropped into a weekday. I didn't do much sleeping, but I did a hell of a lot of staring at my phone and waiting for a sign.

Emptiness is a funny mistress. It picks away at the wrinkles of your brain, tiny pieces at a time, patiently waiting to touch just the right nerve and make everything implode. But until that moment it's like sweeping for landmines, stepping carefully and ripping out all conscious thought until it is replaced by eras of black space; like a river.

I blamed myself a lot that night.

Hoping for the best on Monday, I sat in the Cedar Lounge with a pile of textbooks and the watchful eye of Lance. I ordered a breakfast sandwich and some hash browns to keep him from kicking me out for loitering, and in exchange, I got in about a half hours' worth of studying and two hours' worth of worrying.

"Lance, you seen Bishop at all today?" I dropped my pen in the crease of my textbook, unable to resist the temptation any longer.

"Trouble in paradise?"

"Ugh," I groaned. "Never mind."

Lance placed his dishcloth on the back bar and leaned over, conceding.

"What's wrong, Tee? Need a shot?"

I laugh.

"Lance, it's eleven in the morning."

"Your loss. At least tell me what's going on?"

"You don't even go here, what do you understand about all this university bullshit?" I don't mean to spit out the curse word, but it slid smoothly across my lips to meet the bartender's ear.

"I did go to university once upon a time, Talia." He said this poignantly, very matter-of-fact, as if I were stupid for not considering it. I probably was, but I knew I had more ammunition to play with.

"They have a university for bartenders?"

"Fuck you, I have a business degree."

Well then.

"From here? Shit, glad I didn't go into business." I toyed with him, and the interaction held a strange and familiar warmth. Lance threw his dishcloth at me, but it missed, sopping the floor.

"To answer your question, no, I haven't seen Bishop. He's not usually in here without you guys though."

"Fair, thanks." I chucked the cloth back over the bar, and it disappeared into a mass of bottles, fumbling over Lance's fingers.

As I watched him retrieve it, I texted Michael in my peripheral vision, knowing he and Bishop were in the same morning philosophy class.

Mike, you seen B?
    Nope - didn't show up for class this morning.

There was a little twinge in my stomach just then as I got a horrible feeling. The pieces started falling together in my brain: the bike was gone, he went to see Gemma, and he was never seen again.

All signs pointed to Gemma, and those signs read one word—abandonment.

I don't know why I never fought for Bishop. I guess in some subconscious way I knew that our relationship would never be the same. Something had shifted with the tides, the watery backdrop of us ebbing and flowing until it could be no more. As a result, the week trickled on, a pinhole in a faucet, leaking suspicion and wide-awake nights into my subsistence. The mania of having Bishop coming, careening, into my life had been abruptly halted.

The assumption that Bishop had gotten what he wanted and gone back to Gemma came to me in the wee hours of a morning I can't remember, melding in with all the other days I had spent looking for him. Something ate at me and told me that they had run off to resume their pretty life together with wedding plans and whatever else he hadn't told me. There was only so much you could learn about someone in a month, and clearly, I hadn't learned quite enough about Bishop to realize that maybe he was haunting my life more than enhancing it.

It was a vile, nauseous thought, but one that stuck with me until Tuesday when I was finally able to ascertain what had happened.

I was leaving Professor George's class in the Lamey Building after our semi-regular Tuesday pop quiz when Professor Wyatt stopped me in a crevice halfway down the hall. He appeared as if out of nowhere, his ticked jacket blending in with the crowds of plaid shirts and muted sweaters donned by the student body. He wasn't tall, but he wasn't short, so he melded in with the group expertly, something I felt I had never been able to accomplish with my seemingly towering height as a woman.

"Miss Anderson," he called my name out amidst the chatter of the corridor, and I picked it up before it dissolved entirely.

"Professor Wyatt," I responded, trying to use my least aggravated and most professional tone. I gave him a cursory nod, clenching my textbook to my chest, knuckles whitening with my radiated tension. He looked around before beginning the conversation, as if to evaluate the present company.

"I understand you've been poking around looking for Mister Gale. I have to admit I'm a little bit disappointed. I thought my employment offer would make you reconsider."

"You are aware Bishop's been missing for days?" I asked the question, already expecting a particular answer.

"Why didn't you call the police?"

Wyatt was toying with me, and I didn't appreciate it. However, the inquiry would have been valid if I didn't understand the tone and inflection that came along with it.

"You know where he is, don't you?" I spoke the words as if I were in slow motion.

For the moment, there was no verbal exchange, a hiss filling the air as the groups of students thinned out into classrooms or left the building. Then Wyatt chuckled, a deep, throaty, and menacing sound.

"Of course, I know where he is. I keep appropriate tabs on all my investments."

"Investments?"

Wyatt looked smug. The term had caught me just the way he was hoping.

"Based on your unfamiliarity with the word, I assume you don't know anything about Bishop's past?"

"We were just getting to know each other. Plenty of time for that."

"Not anymore. We've managed to change his mind about you."

I practically stomped my foot like a child, frustrated, dropping my text and corresponding notebook on the ledge beside us. In a valiant attempt at intimidation, I crossed my arms along the fabric of my shirt, knowing I was not at all succeeding.

"Enough of this, Professor. Where's Bishop?"

Wyatt smirked at me, as if he were pleased he had gotten under my skin. Something in that expression told me that my answer wasn't going to come as easily as I'd hoped.

"Bishop's family … the Gale family … is very important to the history of this institution, Miss Anderson. Back when Fischer-Fleming University was built, Dorian Gale was legal counsel to Johnette Wyatt-Fischer and Phineas Fischer." Professor Wyatt paused at that point, either gauging my stupidity or proclivity for keeping up with a conversation.

I must have satisfied him in some way, as he continued. "In part of the agreement for the signing of the ownership to the university, it was decided that a male member of the Fischer family must always remain as head of the board. Pending no suitable individual, a male member of the Gale family may step in for the position on a temporary basis. The only condition being that member had to have obtained, or be in the process of obtaining, a degree from the university."

I nodded, the story making some sense so far; however, the relevance totally lost. My patience was waning quickly.

"Without a degree, the position would follow to the Wyatt family. The eldest male member of Johnette's descent."

He stopped and stared at me. Ten seconds passed. Then twenty. And twenty more until I couldn't stand it.

"What's your point?"

I knew this was all going over my head, except for the familiarity of the surnames being thrown about.

Wyatt sighed, annoyed with my naiveté but amused with his candor.

"Miss Anderson, how obvious do I have to make this story for you to understand? Bishop is the eldest eligible Gale. He supersedes me, as Johnette's eldest inheritor, in the position for the board. That is, if he can actually manage to complete the degree requirements. Which I guarantee, now he can't."

There was a sinister tone to Professor Wyatt's voice as he slipped out the last sentence, something venomous in his dialect. The fluorescent light above my head hummed in an ominous fashion; another omen.

"What did you do to him?"

"Me? Nothing. It offends me you think I'd have something to do with this all. Mister Gale has unfortunately sustained some serious injuries from a motorcycle accident. Pity he was driving the bike in such awful weather."

"What did you do to him?" The words seethed through my lips a second time, oozing perfunctory syllables that were wet with raging hormones.

"I said nothing, Miss Anderson."

"I get the feeling that, with you, nothing means you've done something awful."

His smile made me sick to my stomach.

"Stop worrying about him, Talia. He's Gemma's problem now. Our family will take good care of him. He is a Gale, after all. We have an understanding."

I wanted to scream, but I managed to hold in all of my anger, internalizing it into a steaming, smoking blue fire that burned my insides.

"Where is he?"

Wyatt was unaffected by the caustic feeling in my eyeballs.

"Room 314 at Rose Memorial Hospital. You're welcome to go and visit."

Rose Memorial Hospital was an out of place building in the center of town, tall brick and mortar at odds with the rest of the city and their veneered placards. Aged coal smoke blackened the exhaust tower on the north side edge, faded from years of non-use and the induction of electric heat. On the south side, new windows of full-length glass graced administrative offices and the cafeteria, giving an imprisoned look at the world out of doors, passing the inhabitants by.

The thought of Bishop in there depressed me. But it also sucked me in, thinking of him in some outdated room filled with people he didn't know. Because of this, I didn't wait any time at all to visit, dropping my things off at my apartment before skipping my afternoon classes.

The transparent doors of Rose Memorial slid open as I walked up to them, blowing heated air up at the soles of my feet through a floor-based register. Snow stomped off feet and melted as people shimmied and stepped around me, all of them seemingly knowing where they were headed. While I knew I was headed to 314, I had difficulty processing the directions. My brain felt like it had been run through a washing machine spin cycle.

I gave my head a serious shake, trying to clear away the debris, and followed a series of brightly color-coded signs to the elevator. The call button shone a depleted red, tired after years of being pushed time and time again.

Room 314 was to the east of the hospital, overlooking the back parking lot with a view of downtown. If I had the ability to lift the building up and shift it a little bit to the right, I probably would have been able to spot the dormitories of Fischer-Fleming out the far windows. I was glad I couldn't see any part of the school. Wyatt was there, and I didn't want to even begin to think about him and what he might have had a part in.

I didn't have far to walk down the corridor before I saw the door to Room 314 was open, the bed closest to the hallway empty, but the curtain was drawn around the one farthest away. My hands started to shake, an immediate and anticipatory action, the blood draining from the tips of my fingers and making them prickle.

"Bishop?" I said his name as if I expected his usual response, subliminally hoping for the entire ordeal to be an elaborate hoax. I knew it wasn't, but my entire body ached for a different answer, just as my entire body would suffer the moment I caught a glimpse of what was left of Bishop.

I poked my head around the yellow curtain, eyes taking a moment to adjust and absorb before they landed on the heap under a collection of blankets and tubes. The muscles in my legs immediately atrophied, and I grasped the sheet to keep myself from falling to the floor.

"Gemma?" A crackling voice constructed the word, broken and slow and pained.

"No, Bish. It's Talia."

Silence.

I traced my steps carefully along the tiles, doing my best impression of someone who wasn't falling apart. The truth was that I was on the edge of complete annihilation, an adept hatred for Wyatt pitting my stomach. Tears burned my eyes, clogging up my vision so that when I finally made it to Bishop's bedside, I was looking at the world from under water.

The tears dripped down my cheeks, a rainfall on a misty autumn. Then I could see clearly.

Machines dripped and beeped and counted and dispensed at Bishop's bedside, his face contused with scrapes and his hair bandaged up in astringent white gauze. His hands were mangled into swollen red appendages, his right hand and arm covered in plaster, while the left held an intravenous system. The lower half of his body was hidden underneath his gown and the bleached white of the hospital sheets, likely in a similar state of destruction as the top.

"Gemma?"

I took a seat in a padded flowered chair and scooted it to the bedside.

"No, Bish. I'm Talia."

He smiled, his hazel eyes sparkling, and for a second I was fooled into thinking that he understood me. I wasn't so lucky.

"They took off my ring. They took it off. I meant to have it on." He was babbling, a minor agitation. "I put it down on the table. I didn't lose it. They took it off."

"What? Bishop, what ring?"

Then I saw it on the bedside table. A platinum wedding band, a tiny inscription carved on the interior. Instinctively, I rewound my glance to his left hand, spotting the telltale indent on his third finger.

They were married, and who knew when it happened.

"Our wedding ring, Gemma. It won't fit right now." He closed his eyes and sighed, the counting machine on his right abruptly halting its red alerting light.

"When did we get married, Bee?" I used the nickname as if I needed to convince him I was Gemma, even though there was no reason to assume that. He was barely conscious of my presence, and had yet to acknowledge that I wasn't someone else.

"Before I got hit by the car."

"When did you get hit by a car?"

"It was a black SUV. It hit me. I was hardly moving."

"Bishop, what are you talking about? Are you and Gemma married? Wyatt said you got in an accident from riding that goddamn bike in the snow."

A tingling crimson crawled through my ribcage, knotting in my throat.

"Gemma, I'm tired. Let's talk when I get home."

"No, Bishop, please. Please answer my questions." I begged; an awful, petty sound that did nothing to improve the situation. "Bishop? Come on, please." Salty tears began to collect in my eyes as I leaned back in the chair to admit my own defeat.

They had to have been married this entire goddamn time.

I wanted to throw myself at Bishop, pound his chest and his tattoos in a tympanic destruction, just as his medication induced words were deconstructing all of my feelings. I wondered how long he would live if I unplugged the machines, contemplated leaving a nasty note for Gemma and Wyatt on the wall in permanent marker.

They were married.

He'd made me feel something I never knew was possible, and he was married.

I wished I owned the black SUV that hit him. In that moment, I probably would have smashed into his bike a couple of extra times, just to make sure.

There was no point staying at the hospital. Nothing I could do would bring Bishop around and plus, the more times he called me by Gemma's name, the more frequently my heart was wrenched from my chest cavity. He never picked up that I wasn't a little busty redhead, but instead a lanky blonde with dark circles and a small ass. I didn't bother peeking at his chart to figure out whether he had brain damage or not, the wrapping around his head told me that the fall was serious enough to mess him up.

I thought about pumping some more morphine into Bishop's body as I turned to leave, a sympathetic expression I reserved only for a couple of seconds. The machine was right there, so close and within arm's length, but there was something about drugging him more than he already was that seemed on the verge of illegal. So, I didn't. I closed the curtain and left Room 314, headed down the hall to the elevator, and pressed another exhausted call button.

I arrived back at the ground floor only an hour after I had entered. Somehow the time didn't seem to have moved that far.

Walking down one of the city side streets, I thought about taking a detour to Bishop's house to check on things. I knew there wasn't much in a rented home that a college boy would need looking after in particular, so perhaps the internal suggestion was becoming more of a habit than an actual necessity. Taking two steps forward and three steps back, I opted against the journey, my brain exhausted.

The hospital was nearer to my place than Bishop's anyway.

The sidewalks had recently been plowed by city maintenance, the six inches of snow that fell over the course of the early week pushed to the sides of the embankments. A light brown crust had formed over top of the ivory, sullying the purity of the landscape, pollution from passing cars giving the snow a hazy appeal.

I made it about sixty paces down the block when a black Suburban SUV pulled up beside me, a little dented in on the front and an auburn ponytail in the driver's seat.

"Talia Anderson," the voice crooned once the window rolled down. "Heading home from the hospital? I assume my father told you about Bishop's condition?"

"I witnessed his condition for myself, Gemma."

She nodded, not even thinking to ask how I knew who she was.

"You'll stay away from him now, I hope?" It was less of a question and more of a demand, her inflection barely allowing room for consideration.

I crunched some snow under my boots and look at the painted-over scrapes on the vehicle. There was a part of me that would have loved to tell Gemma exactly where to go, but then there was the other part of me that felt absolutely defeated. Wyatt wasn't going to give up unless he got his way, and it didn't seem like Gemma's apple fell too far from that tree.

Then, Bishop's rambling came to mind.

He was hit by a black SUV.

Gemma must have watched the lightbulb turn on in my head, illuminating the mystery that surrounded her possession of Bishop.

"Did you just think I was going to sit around and do nothing? I knew he was fucking around on me and I was absolutely right. My father gave me your student file printout, and I followed him to your place so many days when he told me he was staying late at school."

"Are you guys married?"

Gemma laughed.

"Get in the car, Talia." I hesitated, and she persisted. "Get in."

So, I got in and the door locked behind me. Gemma signaled back out on to the street and pulled away from the curb.

"Bishop thinks we're married. I told him we are, we're going to be, anyway … so I figured why not embellish the truth a little bit. He's brain damaged, Talia. His short-term memory is toast. To be frank, he has no idea you even exist."

Gemma turned down a side street, and I realized she was taking me home.

"I need to know what happened to him."

She snorted, a barnyard sound that caught with phlegm in her throat.

"Motorcycle accident. I told him not to ride that damn thing in the snow."

I sunk back in the seat of the SUV, crossing my arms.

"I see you and your father have your stories copacetic."

"He doesn't want me to go to jail, and personally I'd rather finish my degree than do time. It's just helpful that we're neighbors with the Chief of Police."

I wanted to scream. I wanted to grab the wheel from Gemma's murderous hands and ram the stupid black Suburban into a brick wall and break her pretty face. I wanted to get rid of the feeling in my chest that was my heart being absolutely destroyed, and instead replace it was a contented feeling of revenge.

But I was locked in my own head, sleep paralysis without the sleeping portion.

We pulled up outside my place only moments later, the engine of the SUV idling as a faint snow began to fall.

"Bishop isn't coming back to the school, I assume you know. We have a family estate down in Florida he'll be staying at until I transfer my credits. Don't worry, my father will arrange for exemplary care."

"I'm more worried how someone like you can be so absolutely evil."

Gemma didn't even recoil.

"Depends on your perspective who the evil one is in this situation."

She isn't wrong.

"Now get out of my fucking car, Talia. I never want to see you again."

"I don't particularly have any burning desire to see you either, Gemma," I unbuckled my seat belt and opened the door, letting in a wisp of flurries. "Enjoy your life with your brain damaged pseudo-husband who you ran over with your father's car. You are honestly, truly fucked up."

The door closed with a vengeful slam, shaking half of the block like a low magnitude earthquake. Gemma smirked at me before she drove away, and I flipped her off, giving her the middle finger, but she was a quarter of the way down the street before I managed to react. I debated if she even noticed at all.

It didn't matter. Nothing felt like it mattered anymore.

Maybe it didn't.

I watched the faded shadow of the Suburban turn left at the stop sign at the end of the street, snow swirling, chilling my skin through the thin coat I was wearing. I was frozen to the spot I had stopped on the sidewalk, my boots stuck to the salted cement and my mind just beginning to process what had actually happened with Bishop, Gemma, and Professor Wyatt. The more people who became aware of the situation, the more likely I would be to be caught in Gemma's path of destruction.

So, I walked up the staircase, carefully, flakes brushing from the wooden railing.

It was December. And Bishop and I were over.

The Good Seed

Don Noel

The professor was an afterthought. Even before he arrived for treatment, Robin was worrying how to bear a really smart child—reluctantly concluding that her husband Hod was not the best choice to father outstanding progeny.

Not that she didn't love Hod. She did, completely and thoroughly; had never thought of straying. He was a thoughtful man, tall and handsome, a household helpmeet and a gentle lover, and would be a wonderful father—after the child was born, or at least conceived.

She'd increasingly seen newspaper and TV reports about the changing needs of the workplace. High school diplomas would soon have little value. Before long, college bachelor's degrees might get an applicant job interviews, but probably not good jobs. Employers were increasingly looking for advanced degrees and "critical thinking" skills.

They had agreed that it was time to start a family; she would quit the pill and begin a calendar to track her renewed menstrual cycle. In a book borrowed from the library, she read that it would take a month to resume fertility, or sometimes longer. It was possible, although rare, to resume fertility without having had a period, the book said -- a possible complication that she didn't want to think about.

Hod wasn't what anyone would call an intellectual. He taught high school history primarily to assure the after-school jobs he liked best, coaching almost every sport in its season. She went to most of his games, and patiently enjoyed hearing his next-morning analysis of each contest. On Sundays, she gave him the sports section and had the rest of the New York Times to herself. Apart from his own games and teams and talent recruitment, his favorite dinnertime topics were the Red Sox or Patriots or Celtics.

Thinking to broaden his horizons, she once took him to the art museum. Bad timing. It turned out to feature an exhibit of gays like Mapplethorpe and Warhol. Hod took one look and abandoned her, waiting in the coffee shop while she hastily toured the displays. He refused ever to go back to the museum.

He laughed at her when, in preparation for pregnancy, she foreswore her occasional glass of wine and insisted they have fish twice a week. She'd read up on protecting and nourishing babies' brains in utero: avoid alcohol; eat foods rich in omega-3s and DHA.

She wasn't entirely confident that she had the genetic endowment to give a child a major leg up into the cerebral world, but she was sure that Hod didn't. Their children would have to be smart to be successful.

She was a physical therapist at Harmony Acres, an upscale retirement community, helping older men and women make the most of new knees and hips or overcome problems ranging from arthritis to balance.

The 'strength clinic,' Harmony Acres called it, a narrow, long room where she worked with two other exercise therapists. It was like a small gym, a cold, whitely over-lit, clinical place: balance bars; step machines; padded leather platforms whose height she could adjust for prone exercises; thick foam rubber pads on which people hopped or stepped to flex leg muscles; racks of dumbbells and inflatable balls of every size.

She tried to make up for the daunting array of muscle mechanics with personal warmth. Management called the residents sent to her 'clients,' a word she refused to use. She didn't like calling them patients, either, and did so rarely. Mostly she avoided any such arms-length words by learning and using their actual names.

They responded with equal warmth. Some of them must have seen her as a daughter, and she was glad to play that role. Every one of them must be pretty smart, successful enough in their careers to afford such a place for their golden years. They chatted while she showed them how to stretch or sit or stand or exercise muscles gone flabby.

Perhaps it was Mrs. Appleby who inadvertently prompted the idea. "I was never very good at sports," she told Robin one day. "My mother picked my father for brains rather than brawn. When I earned my Ph.D. at age twenty-three, she told me that it had been a good choice … even if I didn't manage to ride a bike until I was almost sixteen." She laughed cheerfully at herself.

Robin laughed with her. "No regrets?"

"None," Mrs. Appleby said. "Not being an early biker probably spared me a lot of skinned knees. But now I'm sixty and need coaching to be supple enough to try the tai chi class. Show me that move again, please."

'My mother picked my father for brains.' The phrase etched itself into her mind. It was too late to pick a husband for brains, but perhaps not too late to pick a smart father. She woke at night appalled at herself, then rolled over, lulled back to sleep by the thought of children able to make their way in a demanding world. *'My mother picked my father for brains.'*

Robin meant to make a list of candidates, but no other names came to mind after Dr. Zed appeared, signing up for exercises to improve his balance. Younger than many of her patients—perhaps Mrs. Appleby's age—he was almost as tall and good-looking as Hod, and cheerfully personable.

"Good morning, Mr. Zalinsky," she'd said on his first visit. "I'm sure we can find some exercises that will be helpful."

"Please, everyone here calls me Dr. Zed."

"Oh, I didn't realize. You're a doctor?"

"No, no, it's a Ph.D. My full name is Zigmund Zalinsky, but when I was a Rhodes

Scholar at Oxford, my British classmates started calling me Zed."

A Rhodes Scholar, she thought. *Smart.* Aloud: "I think I remember. The British say 'A through Zed,' right?"

"Exactly. When I came home, two Oxford colleagues joined me at Harvard, and when I earned my doctorate, I became Dr. Zed. The moniker has stuck with me my whole life."

He was scheduled in the rehab center twice a week, doing standing exercises at the waist-level bars and leg lifts from the flat platform. By the third session, she'd decided. Dr. Zed was the perfect candidate: a Ph.D. whose progeny might not only have his brainpower but also—a happy bonus -- look quite a bit like Hod!

Although not yet sure how she would manage it, she stopped taking the pill and marked the calendar.

At the third session, she had him wear a thick canvas belt around his chest, one with a long tail and began giving him a gentle shove now and then, at times he didn't expect it. "We want you to instinctively step back or to the side to keep your balance. To protect yourself from falling."

He smiled at her. "What if I fell?"

"That's what the belt is for. I'd catch you."

"You must be stronger than you look," he grinned, but added, "I trust you," and he went back to regaling her with his experiences as a visiting professor in half-a-dozen countries. "France," he said, lingering a moment as he recounted each of them, obviously recalling thumbnail memories. "Spain. Ah, Spain. Germany. Italy. China. India. Incredible India."

"You learned their languages?"

"You bet. Blessed with a good ear, and a determination not to be embarrassed by making mistakes."

"People didn't mind the mistakes?"

"They were pleased to see me trying, and were glad to help."

She woke up that night from a dream in which her first-born son astonished her by speaking French, Spanish, German, Italian, Chinese and Hindi.

Artificial insemination, she had long since decided, wouldn't work. It would be almost impossible to manage without Hod's knowing, and he would be devastated. Better a once-in-a-lifetime tryst, discreetly arranged, here at Harmony Acres. She was astonished at her audacity, more than a little guilt-ridden, but determined.

She looked Dr. Zed up in the retirement community directory: no wife, no one else listed in that apartment. As she'd guessed, just past sixty. Going to the downtown library, carefully perusing the shelves without asking for help, she read up on age and impotence. The professor was young enough to surely be fertile. Fecund, in fact.

And a widower who might even welcome a romantic encounter. She blushed at that thought but began to savor it. *Pick a father for brains.*

Then a problem: A few days after that decisive session, Dr. Zed fell in his apartment, broke a rib, and had to put his visits to the clinic on hold.

Three weeks went by. She began to explore, in her mind, other candidates among the men she was helping with their rehabilitation. None even began to measure up to the professor. She began to worry about that casual phrase in the library book: 'It is possible, although rare, to resume fertility without having had a period.' The thought flashed through her mind that she should have Hod wear a condom for a few weeks, but she immediately knew that was impossible.

Then, on Friday—oh, joy— Dr. Zed phoned, ready to get back into it. "Just leg and balance exercises," he said. "My ribcage is still painful."

"I understand," she said, digging into her purse for her fertility calendar. *Perfect!* On the most likely scenario, the book described, her ovulation should begin Saturday, so she should be fertile all next week. "How about Monday at ten?"

"Great. I'll be there!"

There might be a problem at home, though. She and Hod always made love on Saturday nights. Her calculation was that she wouldn't be ready to conceive until Sunday at the earliest, but the book said the science was less than exact.

A problem easily solved. "How about dinner out?" she said as soon as he got home from coaching the football team. "There's a band at the hotel restaurant that plays oldies, perfect for dancing. I want to dance with you."

He was a marvelous dance partner, one of the reasons she loved him. By mid-evening, she couldn't wait to get him into bed. At home, she daubed on a touch of his favorite perfume. He fumbled her clothes off like a teenager, and then became the patient lover, his skillful foreplay lasting so long that they were both in ecstasy as they came together.

Afterward, she felt a twinge of guilt, being so calculating; but she thought he was now sated for the week ahead—a week that she was reserving for better seed.

Monday morning, at the rehab, Dr. Zed declared his rib nearly healed, but painful if he coughed. His doctor said he could go back to exercise with her if they were careful.

"The cough pain means your chest muscles have tightened up to protect the ribcage," she told him. "We don't want to do too much until that rib is knitted, but we can begin to loosen up the muscles."

She had him lie down on his back on the therapy platform, and stepped on the pedal to bring it up to waist height. She had him roll onto his side while she folded a towel into a long, soft tube. "Now roll back, so we get that towel under your spine. Good. Can you feel that stretching your chest muscles? Is it painful?"

"De minimus. Only minimally."

Oh, yes, she thought. *He knows Latin, too.* "Nobody speaks Latin," he told her once, "but it's great for vocabulary." She imagined children with vast vocabularies. "Good," she said aloud. "Bring your knees up, please."

"Like that?" For such a remarkable man, he was amazingly compliant with suggestions from a mere exercise therapist.

"Perfect," she said. "Now bend them to the left as far as you can while keeping your shoulders flat. No, no, both shoulders on the mat." She pushed his shoulders down like a wrestler pinning an opponent. "Hold it there ten seconds."

She knew he was counting, but not even moving his lips. Some kind of counter back in that tightly-packed cranium. "Now back up, and bend them to the right. Hold … hold; now back up. How does that feel?"

"Good; I can feel it loosening the chest muscles."

"But not straining the ribs? No sharp pain?"

"No, just right."

She picked out a four-foot exercise rod and handed it to him. "One hand at each end," she said. "Twist as far to the right as you can, until that arm is flat on the mat, or until it hurts, then go back to the other side."

"Like this?"

"But keep your hips flat on the mat. We're trying to make your spine more supple." She thought about pressing his hips down but decided against it.

"All this makes me less likely to fall?"

"Yes."

"Because I'm more likely to be able to catch myself?"

"Exactly." This man had it all scoped out the first time. Most of her patients took weeks to figure it out and do it right. Without prompting, Dr. Zed stretched over to the right, held it ten seconds, then stretched back to the left.

"Does that towel under your spine still feel all right?"

"Yes, just right."

"I'm going to massage your chest just a bit." He was almost as tall as Hod, and it occurred to her that when he was thirty, he probably had pecs as firm and muscular as Hod's. *More good genes.* "We want those tensed muscles to relax so you can pull your shoulders back, or take a deep breath, without discomfort."

"Feels fine, thanks. That's a very gentle massage. I've had masseurs in Istanbul and Djakarta, and other places bear down until it hurt, but felt better afterward."

"We're not doing a real massage," she said. "I can do those, too, but that's not called for here. My, you've traveled a lot."

"Been very fortunate. Probably two dozen countries."

"But didn't learn all their languages?"

"Just enough to say please and thank you and which way is the railroad station." He smiled. "Or the men's room. You like to travel?"

She imagined herself stepping off an airplane in Bangkok to be met by her firstborn son who worked there and spoke the language. "I hope to," she managed. "Can you do this at home?"

"You mean the towel under my spine? I think so."

She'd planned for this. "Tell you what," she said, "I know where to get a shaped foam pad that's just right for this exercise, rather than just a rolled-up towel. I can bring it to you tomorrow. What time are you up and about?"

"Oh, you needn't do that. I can come up here again."

"No trouble at all, Dr. Zed. My parking spot is quite near your end of the complex," she lied.

"Really? That's good of you. I'm through breakfast and reading the newspaper by eight."

"Great. See you in the morning."

⊱ ✦ ⊰

She had to drive across town to get the foam pad, so was late home and preparing Hod's dinner. "Just had to work late," she lied.

"You all right, Robbie? You've seemed distracted lately. Are you pregnant already?"

"No, no just preoccupied." She hesitated, amazed at how readily her brain invented a pretext. "I have a new patient, an eighty-year-old woman who's just gotten a new hip and is afraid to push herself."

"No pain, no gain, right?" Hod often enough had youngsters with strains or pains or even breaks that he understood this part of her work. "Early bed tonight?"

Oh, God. "I have to work on a report. Management wants to be sure we're putting in our time productively."

"Okay. Tell me when I can help."

Dear, sweet Hod. She hunched over the computer after they did the dishes. Blessedly, he turned in soon. He was the kind of sleeper who, once under, couldn't be roused by fire alarms, but she nonetheless crept into bed cautiously. Happily, he didn't stir. It took her a long time to sleep, though. Her mind was racing with scenarios for the morrow.

She contrived not to let Hod see, as she made him breakfast, that she was a nervous wreck. She got him off to work, then dashed back upstairs for a quick shower, examining herself carefully in the mirror before putting on the bra with extra padding and a pants-suit that flattered her figure. One with Velcro instead of hard-to-undo snaps or buttons.

She spent the whole drive from home to Harmony Acres going over the scenarios she'd imagined at night, trying to decide how she might best begin this—what should she call it?—calculated seduction.

She would get him on his bed—on the floor? no, better on the bed—and take elaborate care to be sure that the pad fit the small of his back perfectly. Have him do the exercises he'd done yesterday. Be solicitous that the not-yet-healed rib not complain.

Do a little massage. Maybe more than a little. Lean in, so that her carefully-enhanced breasts were close to his chest. To his face.

She parked, daubed on some of the perfume she'd brought from home, squared her shoulders and headed to the entry door nearest his apartment, the new foam pad in hand.

As he'd told her, his apartment was just down the hall from the entry. She took a deep breath and rang the doorbell.

"Good morning, Dr. Zed."

"Oh, Robin, you're so thoughtful. Please come in. Let me turn down the radio."

Which gave her a moment to take in his digs. The walls of the little living room were hung with prints, some immediately familiar: Mapplethorpe and Warhol, the ones she'd seen at the art museum. Other photos and prints. All of men; no women. On a small table was a bronze statue, which she recognized as a careful replica of Michelangelo's David, full-frontal naked, chiseled pecs and abs, and genitalia.

Prominent behind the little sofa was an oil painting that was obviously an original, a handsome man, tall, greying, surely close to Dr. Zed's age. She stared, as a new reality began to percolate into her consciousness.

He turned and saw her looking at the painting. "My partner of more than three decades," he explained. "He died three years ago."

"I'm sorry for your loss," Robin stammered. She held up the foam pad. "Here's your spine-stretcher."

"Oh, thank you! Can I offer you a cup of coffee?"

"No, thank you. I'd better get upstairs to work."

Contributors

Nicole Bea

Nicole Bea is a short story author, poet, and freelance writer who began pursuing professional writing in 2017. When she isn't coming up with ideas for romance novels, antonyms for the word 'said,' or atmospheric language to describe the world around her, she can usually be found wrapped in a pile of blankets avoiding domestic chores.

She and her husband share their home in Eastern Canada with a collection of disabled cats and a lifetime worth of books.

Please visit her online at www.nicolebea.com

Brandon French

Brandon French is the only daughter of an opera singer and a Spanish dancer, born in Chicago sometime after The Great Fire of 1871. She has been (variously) assistant editor of Modern Teen Magazine, a topless Pink Pussycat cocktail waitress (that's another story!), an assistant professor of English at Yale, a published film scholar, playwright and screenwriter, director of development at Columbia Pictures Television, an award-winning advertising copywriter and creative director, a psychoanalyst in private practice, and a mother.

Fifty-three of her stories have been accepted for publication by literary journals and anthologies, she's been nominated twice for a Pushcart, she was an award winner in the 2015 Chicago Tribune Nelson Algren Short Story Contest, and she has a published collection of poetry entitled "Pie."

Don Noel

Retired after four decades' prizewinning print and broadcast journalism in Hartford CT, he received his MFA in Creative Writing from Fairfield University in 2013.

Don's work has so far been chosen for publication by Calliope, Shark Reef, Drunk Monkeys, The Tau, Indian River Review, Midnight Circus, Oracle, Clare Literary Magazine, The Raven's Perch, Chronicle, The Violet Hour, Literary Heist, Dime Show Review, Yellow Chair Review, Meat for Tea, The Penmen Review, 99 Pine Street, BLYNKT Magazine, KYSO Flash, The Raven Chronicles, Route 7

Review, Halfway Down the Stairs, The Icarus Anthology, Darkhouse Books, Simone Press and of course, Zimbell House.

Catherine J. Wright

Catherine is a world traveler who enjoys warm weather, candlelit dinners, and late nights.

A Note from the Publisher

How to Thank a Contributor

Dear Reader,

Everyone at Temptation Press would like to thank you for reading *The Professor*. If you would like to thank a particular contributor, the best way is to leave a review for them. You may do so by leaving one on our Goodreads page, under the title, *The Professor*, by using the link below: **http://www.goodreads.com/TemptationPress** and be sure to mention the contributor directly.

Why leave a review? Reviews help budding authors build their credibility in the book industry. By posting a review on Goodreads, you help other readers find new authors they may wish to follow, and you never know, your review may end up on an author's website one day.

Friend us on Goodreads:
https://www.goodreads.com/TemptationPress

Visit our website:
http://www.TemptationPress.com

Other Works from Temptation Press

Summer Fling: Tales of Seduction

Kiss & Tell

Coming Soon
from Temptation Press

Choices

Dreams Can Come True